Can't Help Falling in Love

Carol Dunitz and David W. Menefee

MPI
MENEFEE PUBLISHING, INC.
Dallas, Texas, USA

Can't Help Falling in Love Copyright © 2013 Carol Dunitz and David W. Menefee. Adapted from *Already Spoken For* by Carol Dunitz, Copyright @ 1995, published by The Last Word, Ann Arbor, MI.

All rights reserved. No part of this book may be reproduced or distributed, in print, recorded, live, or digital form, without express written permission of the copyright holder. Excerpts of up to 500 words may be reproduced if they include the following information, "This is an excerpt from *Can't Help Falling in Love* by Carol Dunitz and David W. Menefee. For permission, contact either Carol Dunitz cdunitz@bernhardtonbroadway.com or (312) 523-4774, or David W. Menefee PO BOX 181662 Dallas, TX 75218

All photographs and illustrations are from the personal collection of David W. Menefee.

All excerpts are used in editorial fashion with no intention of infringement of intellectual property rights. This is a work of fiction. Names, characters, places and incidents either are products of the author's imagination or are used fictitiously. Any resemblance to actual events or locales or persons, living or dead, is entirely coincidental.

ISBN-13: 978-1480257467
ISBN-10: 148025746X

Chapter One

Allison loved driving in her new cherry red 1954 Chevy BelAir convertible, and this cool, crisp autumn morning offered the perfect opportunity to put the top down. The sky was clear and crystal blue. The nippy air was exhilarating and the wind blew her long wavy red hair. She admired the beauty of the trees as she whizzed past them. Some were already barren, yet others retained the vibrant crimsons, rusts, and yellows in their leaves. Nature's beauty never failed to awaken her ardent passion for life.

Women aren't supposed to get as excited as a man about a car, she mused, *but this is the first car I've ever bought that hasn't been used, and I love tooling around in it! Besides, it has all the bells and whistles that I've ever dreamed of, and it's fun to drive!*

Allison pulled her favorite peach-colored suede coat tight at her neck to block the biting wind. The coat never failed to earn compliments, and she had always looked good in reds and oranges. They highlighted her hair and exquisitely fair complexion.

She turned onto a winding street that led to a new industrial park, where her typesetter had relocated several months earlier. She had been working with Bill, the owner, since she started in the marketing business about a year ago, and he had shown her the ropes. Having grown up in Memphis, he knew who was best at everything, and she valued his tutoring. In many ways, he reminded her of her father, Andrew Webster, who had dominated the Memphis advertising world for years before advancing to a new position managing national advertising for *The Ed Sullivan Show* in New York.

Allison had boldly decided to open up her own office as soon as she was out of college. Having grown up in the business, she believed, perhaps foolishly, that her know-how would bolster her success from the start, but offering her services to small businesses that could not afford to retain the large firms in town had proved challenging.

The concept had been good, but the going was rough—particularly this first year. She discovered that success took more than a good education, talent, and a father in the business. Being the daughter of a locally prominent ad man opened some doors, but now she had to succeed by her own talent and wits, or fail. She had to be as self-assured as a pro, be willing to work extra hard, and be able to take an aggressive stance with members of the business community. She had been willing to make the necessary commitment. She was weathering the lean times and earned a few kudos, but she could not pay the electric bill with kudos. She had to grow her small but challenging list of clients.

I've got to secure some new clients! she thought, as she approached the large, gray brick building where Bill had his shop. She squeezed into a small space near the road, and then rushed to the entrance with one hand holding tight to her purse and briefcase. With the other, she pushed the door open and scooted inside.

Bill was in the outer office discussing a job with Mark, one of his employees. Both men were perched on stools and engrossed in some rough layouts spread out on a table.

"Brrr!" Allison said, feeling a chill dance up her spine and down her arms. She set her things down while hanging her overcoat on a brass rack by the door. "It's unseasonably cold for mid-September, isn't it Bill?"

Bill stood up to heartily greet her. His six-foot two-inch, 250-pound frame immediately dominated the entire room. "Good morning!" he said. "We haven't seen much of you this past week. Glad you stopped by. We're just finishing up here."

"Oh, don't mind me. If it's okay with you, I'll just check my phone for messages while you two finish. Can I use your phone?"

"You know you don't have to ask," Bill reassured her. "There's coffee and donuts in the back if you want some."

Allison straightened out the bow of her blue silk blouse and pulled her tweed suit jacket back into place before crossing to the far side of the room and placing her purse on the coffee table. Both men watched her after she passed, admiring her fresh, wholesome appearance. She felt their eyes on her. She enjoyed the fact that men appreciated the effort she took to present a feminine yet businesslike image. At twenty-four, love was something Allison considered precious, particularly because love had eluded her, so far. She reached for the coffee pot and surveyed the donuts. *It'll take more than admiration from co-workers to keep me happy. It takes love. I wonder if I'll ever meet Mr. Right. He sure isn't anywhere in the world of advertising!*

She could hear Bill picking up where he had left off when she came in. When she returned with a mug of black coffee and a glazed donut, the two men were so involved with their work that they had tuned her out. She pulled out a ring binder from her leather handbag, quickly reviewed the notes she had made the preceding day, and then reached for the wall phone and dialed her answering service.

"This is Allison Webster. Do you have any messages for me this morning?"

"One moment please. Miss Webster, there's just one message."

"Just one? Please read it to me."

"A man called wanting to see you. The morning girl took the call and her handwriting's terrible. I can't quite read his name. It looks something like Alvin, Elton, Elrod, or something like that . . . ."

"Go on."

"That's all there is."

Allison tried not to show her annoyance, but she had to carp, "What do you mean that's all? If he said he wanted marketing help, he'll be a new client for me. I'll need a last name and a number!"

"The morning girl didn't get a last name. I'm so sorry!"

"This is the second time she's done this to me!"

"I'm sorry."

Allison sighed and licked the nub of her pen. "Okay, read me his number." She carefully copied down the numerals, but then she sensed that Bill and Mark were watching her, and she looked up.

Bill chuckled, even though he was intrigued. "Looks like you may have hit the jackpot, little lady! It sure would be terrific to start the week off with a new client!"

"If you don't want him," Mark said, "send him to us. We'll take all the new business we can get!"

Allison spoke with guarded enthusiasm. "Now fellas, let's not get all excited about this before I find out what this mysterious new prospect with no last name actually called about. It may be nothing!"

Bill quickly retorted. "Then again, it could be the start of something big! Why don't you go back in my private office and return the call? But first, calm down!"

"You're both right. I'm grateful for any new business. It's just that I like to make a good first impression when I approach a new prospect, and it's hard to springboard to perfection when the girl at the call center can't even give me a clue who he is!"

Bill teased, "You're perfect the way you are."

She winked at him and said, "But I can be a witch before my morning coffee, especially when I have to call someone I don't know who contacted me from out of the blue!"

With her appointment book in hand, she took advantage of Bill's offer to tuck herself away in his private work space. As she closed the door, she turned around and her jaw dropped. Papers were strewn all over every surface. She was hard-pressed to find a spot amidst the appalling clutter to even set down her things. A manual typewriter veiled in an inch of dust sat forlornly to one side of the desk. Unmailed invoices were piled in his chair. Half-eaten sandwiches and soft drink bottles dotted the tops of every file cabinet. Bill's office looked as if the room had been struck twice by a tornado.

Allison sighed and pulled his chair up to a drawing board positioned at a right angle to his desk. She restacked his invoices in a neat pile and sat. *How can I best present myself to this mysterious potential client with no name? He probably wants me to make a presentation to him, but how did he come to call me?*

She picked up the telephone and started to dial him, but before the connection was made, she hung up. She was uncharacteristically nervous. *Why am I so jittery?* she wondered. *What makes this message so different from any other message I've gotten lately? Allison, regain your composure and call him now!*

She dialed again and a gravelly-voiced older woman answered, "How can I help you?"

"My name's Allison Webster with Webster Marketing. Someone named Alvin or Elrod called me. I hope he's still in."

"No one by those names works here. This is the Bon Air Club."

"The Bon Air Club?"

"Call back around nine o'clock. You might catch him then."

Allison was taken aback. "Nine o'clock tonight? Did you say he's *playing there*? Is he a performer?"

"Me, the comics, and the bands are the only people who use this phone, honey. If it's one of them and you're in the marketing business, he'll probably want to talk to you."

"Would you leave a note that I called? I'll try to call back."

"Sure thing, honey." With that, the connection went dead.

Allison chided herself. *Why didn't you try to get more information? Why didn't you manage to ask any pertinent questions like you usually do? I wonder what he wants anyway. Doesn't sound like a big-time client prospect. There aren't any big headliners at the Bon Air Club!*

After finishing her business with Bill, Allison returned to her office and spent the entire afternoon reading her weekly copy of *Advertising Age* and flipping through pages of a new book on retail advertising that she had recently bought. She even toyed with the idea of going to the Bon Air Club in person, but decided against it. *What if I can't even get to him? The whole trip would be a waste of time.* She looked up at the clock. 5:45. *Oh, he can call me in the morning. Musicians are so unpredictable. This doesn't sound like much of a new prospect!*

She got her coat and was half way out the door when she remembered her briefcase. *No,* she insisted to herself, *I'm not taking any work home with me.* She sighed, closed the door, and heard the latch lock.

A few steps down the hall, she heard the telephone ring from inside. She scurried back, unlocked the door, and flew inside, barely managing to grab the phone without dropping her purse. "Hello? Allison Webster speaking."

"Miss Webster?" The man's voice sounded deep, soft, and southern. "I didn't know if you'd still be in, but . . . I'm the guy who called you from the Bon Air Club. I'd like to spend some money with you. You see, I need your help."

Chapter Two

"I was sort of hoping I could get an appointment with you," the performer asked. "I've heard some good things about you. I'm sorry that things have been kind of hectic lately, but I want to talk to you."

"Are you wanting to talk to me about marketing?"

"Yes ma'm . . . sort of."

For a moment, Allison hesitated. He sounded sweet but vague, more like a boy from the country, not the kind of hard-nosed businessman she usually encountered. But she quickly reverted to her professional demeanor and said, "Let me check my schedule."

"I—I'll be out of town for the rest of the week. How would a week from today—that is—next Monday work out?"

"I'm afraid next Monday is out of the question," she replied. "I do have Tuesday morning wide open, though. How's nine thirty?"

"Fine, I guess. I'll see you then. If you're around the Lamar-Airways Shopping Center tomorrow at noon, come by. I'll be playing there. Bye."

"Do you mind if I ask—"

Before she could say more, he hung up.

Is he a musician or a comic? she asked herself. *He didn't crack any jokes, and he sure didn't sound like he'd be any threat to Perry Como. But there was something . . . something in his voice . . . the timbre and tone. I've heard that voice somewhere!*

The next morning, Allison did a little checking up on the Lamar-Airways Shopping Center event. She learned that a band *was* going to play there and the lead singer was a guitar player that the locals enjoyed. He had a style that reminded some people of Black rhythm and blues singers, a startling contrast to the norm. He wore his hair in a huge pompadour slicked up with rose water and Vaseline, and he sometimes performed in shocking bright-colored suits. Some people had said that he struck poses that were alarmingly indiscreet, while others found him luridly ingratiating. Allison felt intrigued and somewhat fascinated by him, and she decided to go see him for herself.

Finding a parking place proved more challenging than she imagined. Although the band had apparently been playing small gigs in and around Memphis, they were the center of attention at the Grand Opening that day. More than a hundred girls and an equal number of teenage boys descended on the parking lot where a makeshift stage had been erected. By the time the music show began, the impatient throng seemed to have more than doubled. Allison was notably impressed by their enthusiasm and excitement, however the band's singer bore no resemblance to the seemingly mild and polite man she had briefly spoken to on the telephone.

The band was loudly amplified by two big speakers. A couple of teenage girls were pressing in on Allison's left and she overheard one of them say, "We've got to go see him at the drugstore after the show!"

After their squealing calmed down a bit, Allison leaned nearer and said, "Excuse me . . . did I hear you say that he'll be making an appearance after the show?"

"At the Katz Drugstore!"

"Where's that?"

The girl giggled. "Right across the street!"

Allison looked to where the girl pointed and said, "Thanks!" She glanced back at the stage and decided, *I'm going over there now. If I can get up close enough, maybe I can . . . . no! I won't try to talk to him today. That'll make me look too pushy, even though he did invite me to come down. Besides, there are too many people to have a meaningful talk. I already have an appointment to meet him face to face Tuesday morning. I'll wait until then, even though I want to see him now!*

She lingered a while longer. The music, the beat, his voice, and his wild movements soon merged into an infectious, primal enticement that ensnared everyone in the audience. Allison could not help but notice how the young throng literally swayed with the tunes, and at one point, she caught herself moving along with them, a trifle matter that left her surprised and more than a little embarrassed.

She tried to understand why she was reacting that way and felt defensive. *The fact is that a show business performer could become an extremely lucrative client. But he's, after all, only one account. Still, none of my other clients have ever made me feel this way before! What is it that's so special about him? Maybe it's the glamour and excitement. I shouldn't feel this way. I haven't even met him yet!*

She continued to argue with herself, mostly because of the influence he seemed to be having on her psyche, something akin to the schoolgirl romance from afar that she once had with Frank Sinatra. Still, she could not ignore the fact that she knew enough about him to know "a catch" when she saw one. His photograph—albeit an amateurish-looking one—had graced the pages of the local newspaper more than once during the last few weeks. He was always working at various popular venues in town. He wore the latest clothes, and he was lean and handsome. He could just be a flash in the pan, but he was certainly working in an industry where fame and fortune could reach a pinnacle fast and then spiral into a nosedive, crash, and burn all in a single year. *Maybe he truly needs my help,* she considered.

Allison was bravely determined to obtain a closer inspection of the music hero that had so strongly entrenched his hold on the teenagers at the outdoor concert. When the show ended, she made a beeline to the Katz Drugstore, and none too soon. The area quickly became swamped with more than a hundred giddy girls, all of whom seemed to have the same aim as Allison—to see him up close.

They did not have to wait long for their dreamboat's arrival, but Allison's astute marketing skills clued her in on the fact that his appearance there that day had been strategically plotted to promote the one single record he seemed to have to his credit, which just happened to be readily in stock inside the drugstore in an end cap on the record aisle.

The quartette jumped up on a flatbed truck that had been parked in front of the drugstore, and they performed the A and B sides of their single once, with his band struggling to provide backup without any amplification. The nearly three hundred people—mostly teenage girls—responded with enough enthusiasm to encourage them to sing those same two songs over and over. Allison noted that they seemed to crave the excitement and mood, not the music so much, plus there was a decidedly sexual charge to the atmosphere that was so thick you could cut the voltage with a knife.

Finally, an announcement was made by Sleepy-Eyed John, a local disc jockey. "Maybe this is the first time some of you've had to enjoy these boys. I want to invite all of you to his next date at the Eagle's Nest on Friday night!"

That pronouncement caused the girls to erupt in a deafening roar. Allison had seen and heard enough for now. The horde pressed in on her and she could not get near enough to introduce herself to him. *I might as well go while I can still manage to drive down the street,* she thought. *Now, at least, I can put a face to the name, and he certainly seems to possess a good luck charm that works a spell on these girls. That's for sure!*

The following Tuesday arrived with Allison's alarm clock ringing and nearly rattling off her bedside table. She pressed the off button. Part of her was glad that she would be meeting a possible new client, but part of her dreaded the appointment.

As she lay snug beneath the sheets and drifted in and out of that half-consciousness that always heralded the start of a new day, her thoughts kept drifting to the extremely special appointment she had made. *Here I am fretting about meeting that guy and wishing I didn't have to, when I know there's probably hundreds of other girls right here in Memphis who would give anything to be in my place!*

She chastised herself for dwelling so apprehensively over the matter, and pulled herself from bed. She and her younger sister, Karen, had shared an apartment for about a year. Having grown up together in Memphis, the two of them enjoyed an unusually close friendship. Karen had been on vacation for a week, and the apartment seemed empty without her. Allison found herself wandering about the apartment, peering into her sister's room, and forcing herself to think about surprising Karen by cleaning their goldfish tank—anything to keep her mind from wandering back to that uncomfortably nagging apprehension that hung over her like a dark cloud.

Why does she need to be away just when I really need to talk with her? Allison wondered, miffed. *I might not want to tell Karen anything about this worrisome obsession I'm harboring until I'm sure that I'm completely in control of whatever might be about to happen. It's so very important to be in control, and I feel like I'm being forced to stand afoot on a spinning merry-go-round! I've never felt this way before. It's so uncharacteristic of me, and I don't think I like it!*

The morning passed in a haze of going through the usual motions of dressing. She had plenty of time to bathe and have a leisurely breakfast. She sauntered back into her own room and went over to her closet. She gazed at her clothes and considered the pros and cons of each outfit in her wardrobe. *I should have made a decision earlier what to wear!* she chastised herself. *I think I can safely narrow the choice down to two outfits—the gray ultra suede dress or the red mohair suit. The red mohair suit might be just the ticket. May as well look my very best, businesslike and professional. No sense in showing up in a too-attractive dress that could give him the wrong impression!*

She poured two capfuls of bath oil into the tub and ran a steamy, hot bath. Luxuriating in the water finally soothed her mind until she lost track of the time and nearly fell back to sleep. She languidly glanced at a clock on the wall. *8:30!* She snapped to and sat upright, making a big splash that sent water cascading over the tub to the tile. She swiftly got out, dried off, and sat down in front of her makeup table.

Allison dusted her cheeks with some powder, then a little rouge. After she applied mascara and curled her eyelashes, she sat back for a moment and stared at her reflection in the mirror. She carefully studied her features, mentally commenting on each one before moving to the next. *All-American good looks—large green eyes, slightly turned up nose, and my features are highlighted by a nice complexion. I look attractive, but will he think so? That's what matters!*

She dressed quickly, moving like lightning when she unhesitatingly selected accessories. Then she grabbed her coat, and was out of her apartment and on the way.

She arrived early, hoping that he would extend the same courtesy and at least be on time, but when she darkened the doorway of her office, her jaw dropped. He was already there!

Chapter Three

Marge, the secretary she shared with two other tenants, was an older woman. She started to point him out to her, but Allison had already seen him. He stood and walked over to greet her. She was stunned by his presence. Ah, yes—now she could see what had so charmed the multitudes at his shows. He was handsome in his photographs, but not half as handsome as he was in person. He was taller than she expected—at least six feet—or was the extreme upsweep of his hair what made him seem that tall? She was not sure, and with his gaze seeming to penetrate her soul, she had little time to contemplate his statistics. The closer he came, the more she felt overpowered by his trim, well-groomed appearance and excellent physical shape that he obviously made every effort to maintain. His large blue eyes perfectly complemented his ruddy complexion, and she felt his magnetism before he spoke.

He even smiled divinely. "Morning, Miss Webster. Thanks for letting me come by today." He reached around to help her with her coat. He was so near! For a fleeting moment, she could actually see his long eyelashes clear enough to count them. As his hand grazed her shoulder, she felt a shiver of delight.

"You're not only on time, you're early!" Allison stammered, instantly wishing she had said something cleverer, perhaps a quip that he would remember later. Instead, she stammered, "Please come and sit down."

They moved across the room together to her office. Once there, she motioned to one of two leather love seats positioned facing each other, and only after she sat down did he seat himself on the love seat opposite.

"Would you like some coffee?"

"I sure would, ma'm. I'd love some. I do these shows, and they sometimes keep us up pretty late at night. I rushed over here this morning, so I didn't have time for a cup."

Allison called to her secretary. "Marge, would you please bring in some coffee and sweet rolls?"

He shifted his position. For the first time, Allison noticed a large manila envelope he had placed beside him.

She found herself surprised at how familiar she felt around him. Forgetting all about taking copious notes as she usually did while politely interrogating a new client to determine needs, she slid back into the pillows. Once again, she was struck by the kaleidoscope of emotions swirling through her head and she felt more than a little flushed. *He seems so obviously comfortable, yet I'm still feeling like a thirteen-year-old on my first date! This is ridiculous. I'm supposed to be in charge of the meeting. Say something professional, Allison!*

Before she could pose any questions, he asked, "Have you seen any of our publicity, Miss Webster?" He waited for her reply, but he smiled, and his lip slightly curled.

Allison's mind recalled the black and white coverage she had seen in the newspaper and the not so flattering photograph of him. "A little, recently. Have there been more?"

"No, and that's the problem, you see."

"Is there something about what's been done so far that bothers you?" Now that her professional manner had kicked in, her mind raced ahead while she reprimanded herself. *Of course! That's what this is about! Oh, why didn't I come prepared with research before meeting with him? I could have anticipated his needs and stunned him with some ideas that would perhaps alter the course of his future success.*

"Yes, ma'm. They're just not good enough."

The door opened and Marge entered with a tray on which she carried a coffee pot, two mugs, and assorted jelly donuts.

"Ah, here's breakfast! Thank you, Marge," she said, glad for the momentary distraction so she could regroup her thoughts. "Would you be kind enough to hold my calls until we complete our business?"

Marge sensed that she should make herself invisible, and simply replied, "Yes."

Allison asked, "How do you drink your coffee?"

"Black, please."

She poured their coffee and handed him his mug. "How did you hear about me?"

"From a truck driver friend of mine."

"A truck driver?"

"Yes ma'm. Benny the Dip—he owns a used car lot here—and was talking to me and one of the other guys in the band the other day. Benny drives a big rig when he has time, and he mentioned that you had done some stuff with him. I need your help."

"My agency has done some automobile advertising this year. But we've handled marketing in a number of areas. I could certainly help with music industry promotion. I have some samples on my desk I can show you."

"You don't have to go to all that trouble. If Benny the Dip likes you, then I know I will. I can tell you what I need." He reached for his manila envelope and pulled out a dozen or so tear sheets—samples of press he and his band had received—and spread them across the coffee table. "Look at these articles and ads. They appeared in newspapers this past summer all around the state."

Allison bent over and perused the specimens while he leaned close and followed her gaze. She could barely smell his Raffia Lime. Being that near to him felt so arousing that, for a moment, she held her breath and was afraid to move or speak. *Get a hold of yourself, Allison!* she silently chastised herself. *Ignore him and concentrate on the tear sheets!* But, she had to look at him, and she needed to comment. *His lips are so close to mine!* She gulped noticeably. *Is he looking at me or the tear sheets? He seems to be looking at me!*

She felt the blood rush to her cheeks and was embarrassed that her feelings might be too obvious. For one brief moment, they both looked into each other's eyes a little longer that a man and woman would in any normal situation. Then, he picked up a jelly donut and took a bite. Allison watched him closely. *He's calm, composed . . . and obviously hungry. He's now looking at that donut the same way he just looked at me. Our deep exchange of glances meant nothing to him, or did it? I'm so confused!*

"There's room for improvement, right? Everybody keeps telling me that I've gotta have some great pictures, you know, like the kind you see with James Dean, or Rock Hudson, or Marlon Brando."

Allison was overcome with a desire to hug him . . . in a motherly or sisterly way. He seemed like a big Teddy Bear in need of affection, but she was still wracked by that other surge of emotion coursing through her entire being—a primitive passion laced with ideas that she had to acknowledge were nearly shameful. She gulped when admitting to herself in a flash how uncharacteristic those thoughts were for her to consider. All these emotions swirled through her mind in no more than an instant, yet she could feel her heart pounding and her temperature rising. Now that he had broken the ice and revealed the crux of his concerns, she felt confident that her ability to take charge of the situation and resolve the problem was entirely within reach. *If only he was!* she thought, giving herself over to the capricious urge she was feeling. Then, she heard herself saying out loud, "Memphis may be known as the city of musical invention, but I can assure you that my campaigns—and the photographs we use in them—

are as creative as anything Madison Avenue in New York turns out. It seems as though you've been extremely patient. After all, a poorly planned campaign using a set of unflattering photos can hold you back from success!"

"That's what I've been trying to tell the guys in my band!" he said while obviously relishing his donut. "You and me think alike! I like that about you. Benny the Dip was right!"

"You know," Allison said, "I believe that every client deserves to get his money's worth. Whether you have $1,000 or $1 million to budget for promotion, the money needs to be invested wisely." Allison watched him fascinated. *He never speaks while chewing, but then he swallows big gulps like a German Shepherd. That jelly donut vanished in less than sixty seconds!*

"We don't have either of those figures, ma'm, but you're right. What we have now isn't cuttin' the mustard."

"Clearly, you're not getting what you should be getting from your marketing dollars."

"You're right again, ma'm."

"You can call me Allison. Please . . . ."

"Alright, ma'm . . . uh, Allison. One of these days, we sort of plan to have some hit records. Already, they're asking for pictures, and I don't have any good ones."

"You need more control over your career."

"I do, I mean, we do, that's for sure. We'll be getting a big-time manager, I think, one of these days, and I can already see that I need to have a promoter. You could help all the guys, don't you think?"

He said 'we.' What did he mean by that? Is it this coffee that's setting me on fire, or am I blushing? Allison dismissed the thought that he was thinking of the two of them in any intimate sense because she was already baffled by the ridiculously wild and nearly impossible to suppress fantasies playing havoc with her emotions. "I believe I can, she replied.

"That's why I came here to you. I'd like you to get us on the right track. Now tell me, what do you think would happen if I kissed you right now?"

Chapter Four

"What?" Allison was stunned by his unexpected question, so direct, so shockingly bold that his query could only mean that he had sensed exactly what she had been experiencing for the last five minutes. She stammered, "I imagine that . . . I might like that a lot . . . or I might faint. I'm not sure!"

"All those girls who come to our shows, that's what I want them to wonder when they see a picture of me."

Allison parted her lips, but she was unable to respond. The conversation was ricocheting in too many directions at once.

He leaned forward and added, "Benny the Dip was right. Those ads you did for him—he said they increased his sales and helped put him on the map. You've got what it takes, exactly what we need. How did you do that?"

She felt as if she had stepped outside on a garden rake, only to have the handle swing up and strike her on the head. *So, he absolutely wants me to focus on promoting his career!*

"I'd like you to head things up," he said. "Was it hard for you to help him?"

Now, Allison felt the need for sustenance. Perhaps a jelly donut would calm her down enough to express some professional tips about a campaign or a style of photos that would meet his needs. She reached for the pastry tray. "Would you like another donut?"

He laughed. "Thanks. I didn't want to seem rude, but I'm glad you asked."

"I'll have one, too. No, it wasn't terribly difficult for me because it's what I do professionally. I looked at what his competition was doing right and what they were doing wrong and used that as a springboard for new inspirations.

There's no lawbreaking in copying some elements of a good ad design."

He reached for another donut. "Good, because I want to sort of look the way James Dean looks. Have you seen *East of Eden?*"

"Yes. I can see your point. That would be clever. There's a series of ads running in major magazines right now that are promoting him brilliantly."

"Benny the Dip said I should call you, but he said you were too beautiful for me and there might be sparks."

Allison almost choked on his words. She looked at him with an expression that crossed between surprise and confusion. "You mean you would like me to help?"

"Sure!"

"Now that I've met you, I'm certain I could add value to your campaign." She smiled her most winning smile and carefully considered her next words before she spoke. In front of her sat a man who was on the cusp of fame and fortune, and he had just profusely complimented her. She did not want to offend him, but she did not want to appear desperate for a new client either. "Naturally, I'm flattered," she commenced, "and I think we should get started right away."

He seemed to again inhale his second donut, and he reached for a third. "You're right. It's now or never."

Allison smiled. "When I went into business on my own, I did so because I wanted the freedom that went along with being self-employed. This way, I can choose which projects I want to work on and which ones I don't want to work on. I would enjoy working with you." She had the presence of mind to hold back from revealing her innermost thoughts. *After all, what person in my field wouldn't kill for the chance to help an obviously rising star, albeit a fledgling? What if he and his band really do take off? I hope I'm not biting off more than I can chew!* Allison knew that she was ready to take on this assignment and finally spread her wings. "In short," she continued, "I have more flexibility this way—and although I may have to spend time with my other clients, I'll do my best to give you my undivided attention as often as needed."

His expression became pensive, and he looked at her like James Dean brooding over Natalie Wood. "Good then. I want you to take us on. My first record's getting some play on the radio stations around here, so maybe you can come up with some ideas that'll work."

Allison lit up. "We'll have to proceed quickly. I want to develop and produce promotional material for your appearances. We'll need to spend some time in a studio with a photographer right away. Unfortunately, I don't have more time today. If you have time late tomorrow afternoon, I'd like to meet with you again then."

"Are you free in the afternoon? We'll be at the Eagle's Nest real late tonight, but maybe around four?"

"That'll be fine."

He rose to leave. He gathered his tear sheets up and deposited them back in the envelope. "Miss Webster . . . ."

"Please, call me Allison," she quickly interjected.

"It's been great meeting you. I'll look forward to seeing you tomorrow." They shook hands, and then he turned to go, but he turned back toward her. "Allison . . . ."

"Did you want to take another donut with you?"

"No thanks. Three's enough. Umm, there might be one catch about you being our marketing person."

She noticed that his eyes twinkled as he spoke. "A catch?"

You might think about modeling in some of the pictures. With your hair in a pony tail, you could easily pass for one of the girls in our audiences."

Was he serious? I've never modeled for any magazine ads. "But I'm not a professional model!" she protested.

"But you could be." With that comment, he turned toward the door. "I'll see you tomorrow!"

Allison was speechless. He had again complemented her, but he also bewildered her and dismissed her with the turn of one phrase, not to mention the fact that he had bewitched her with his brooding gaze draped in those mesmerizing long eyelashes, his southern but respectful drawl, his deliciously curled lips that were so near hers, and then . . . that whirlpool of passion he inadvertently stirred up inside her that whirled like a washing machine on spin and then coursed through her veins like hot steam. Because she could not yet organize and digest her entire encounter with him, she merely said, "Goodbye!"

He stopped short of closing the door behind him. "You might get a chance to hear our new record if you happen to be listening to WHBQ around ten o'clock tonight. It's a rhythm and blues song about a blue moon and a love that said goodbye."

He shot her another one of those disarming smiles that sent her head reeling, and then he closed the door behind him.

She sat down again, mentally and emotionally exhausted and struggled to regain her composure. *What had he meant by that? Am I losing my wits because of the rush from the coffee and jelly donut, or am I sensing that there really is more to his feelings about me that he's willing to show? Maybe that seemingly shy and extremely polite exterior hides a deeply-dug well of passion that's just waiting to erupt like volcano magma? I can tell we're just about the same age, so maybe we're both frighteningly caught up in something larger than either of us can imagine? Is this the start of something big, just like Bill said?*

Marge brought her back to reality. "Miss Webster, are you alright? Your face just blanched of all color. You look sick. Do you need a bicarbonate?"

"No, I think I need a priest!"

Chapter Five

Allison arrived at the Memphis airport forty-five minutes before Karen's plane was scheduled to arrive. While she was glad that her little sister was returning home, she would not normally have been so early. As she sat at the gate, the tasks that needed to be attended to came to her mind. She could have worked on more copywriting back at the office. She could have reviewed the layouts her most talented freelancer dropped off that morning. She could even have done something that did not take much concentration, such as stopping at the printer's to check the progress on the completion of a brochure. As always, there was a lot to do, but she could not keep her mind on her work.

All Allison could think about was her new assignment helping promote his band's new record. She was not sure exactly what she would be doing for them yet, but that did not matter. She had a new challenge, and she thought about her meeting that morning with him. *What a wonderful guy!*

Most passengers had deplaned when Karen stumbled through the door from the tarmac and entered the terminal. She looked somewhat disheveled in a flannel shirt and blue jeans that fit a bit tighter than usual. While she was tall and pretty like Allison, she tended to be pleasantly plump compared with Allison's lithe build. Her tight blond curls danced around her face and down the back of her neck, and she wore no makeup. She peered over a hefty armful of packages she juggled while looking for her sister. Karen expected Allison would be there. They always met each other, but Allison was nowhere in sight.

Then, she saw her sitting at the far end of the gate, lost in thought. Little did she know her sister was fantasizing about a handsome and talented musician, totally oblivious that the plane had even arrived. She was caught up in an enthralling daydream about him and the things he had said and insinuated that morning.

How unlike Allison! Karen thought, as she trudged clear across the terminal toward her. *She's usually so down to earth. I wonder what's been going on since I left.*

"Allison! Allison!" Karen called, as she finally stood over her sister. "Come back to this world and help me!" She dropped her packages with a thud that finally jarred Allison back to the present.

Allison jumped up and hugged Karen. "I'm so glad you're home! How was your trip?" She eyed Karen closely, knowing that she had a tendency to dismiss facts and feelings she did not want to deal with. This was to have been an important time for Karen and her boyfriend, Freddie, but the first thing Allison noticed was that her sister had taken off her engagement ring. Allison saw her sister's eyes glass over with tears, and she knew she was upset.

"My trip? Not what I expected. I gained five pounds and blew most of my savings on a shopping spree! I guess I'm just no good at shedding old boyfriends."

The terminal was nearly empty by now of other passengers, so Allison asked sympathetically, "Do you want to talk about it?"

"What is there to talk about? Freddie's been going out with another woman for three months and never even told me! And to think I thought we were going to get married. I must walk around with plugs in my ears and a paper sack over my head at times!"

Allison thought about her sister's uncanny ability to fall in and out of love, so she replied with concern, "Long distance relationships are difficult to sustain. He was geographically undesirable, at best. You'll meet someone new, hopefully someone much nicer!"

Karen smiled faintly through her tears and put on a happy face. She dismissed the uncomfortable topic with her usual, quick style and bent over to retrieve her packages. "You bet I will. I'm not upset. I just retreated into a cookie and cake cocoon and gained five pounds that I'll have to find some way to take off!"

Allison knew not to ask any more questions. She sensed that Karen's relationship with Freddie had been cooling off long before her sister left for vacation. In any case, moving on to other topics seemed best. She was sure that Karen was already thinking and planning about where to find new romance. Karen was like that. She refused to dwell on past hurts and speedily blocked them out of her mind. She liked being in love and had a special knack for getting there.

Allison picked up the rest of the packages, and the two sisters headed for the baggage claim area to retrieve the luggage. She had promised herself she would say nothing about her sensational new client to anyone until after her next meeting with him. However, once she was alone with Karen, keeping secret the fact that she had just met the most exciting guy in years proved too difficult.

"I landed a new project while you were gone," Allison coyly commented, knowing this would provide a fine distraction. "It came like a big Christmas present all tied up with a big red bow and covered with glitter. You'll never guess what was inside the box."

"Something tells me it was more than a cashmere sweater."

"Just a gorgeous man who's the heartthrob of nearly every girl in Memphis right now."

"I suppose he's what you were mooning about when I got off the plane? You looked like Deborah Kerr longing for Burt Lancaster in *From Here to Eternity!*"

"How'd you guess?"

"Come on now, Allison. I may be younger than you, but I wasn't born yesterday. I know when my sister is thinking about something that has her obsessed, and I also know how she looks when she's thinking about a new man. I can tell by the expression on your face. You know, just because my latest romantic relationship went bust doesn't mean you should hold out on me about yours. Fact of the matter is, it'll make me feel good to hear about it. At least there'll be some vicarious thrills today. Now, own up!"

"Karen, it *is* just a new job," Allison replied almost convincingly. They sauntered over to the conveyor belt that would bring Karen's luggage from the plane. Allison hesitated before she went on, knowing so little herself about how the new project was going to play out. She did not want to seem like the matter was sketchy, and she had no desire to tease. So, she decided to simply lay out the facts she had right at the moment. "He just needs some new promotion ideas and photos, that's all. I'm sure nothing could ever happen between us. We travel in different worlds. I'm eight to five, Monday to Friday, and he seems to work odd hours, sometimes late at night and under the craziest circumstances you can ever imagine. I mustn't let myself believe anything could come of it."

Karen was quick to disagree. "Nonsense! How can anything exciting happen if you don't let yourself believe it can? Tell me more about him!"

Allison was glad that Karen mirrored her own giddy sense of shock over the impact the singing dreamboat had made on her. She was dying to spill her secret and her eyes twinkled as she spoke. "I'm sorry, Karen, but I can't. I mean, I could, but it's only mundane things like the fact that he can sing like a dream, has his first record just out, and has that unusual knack of stirring a crowd of teenage girls to a frenzy!"

"Not to mention that he has you looking like a tea kettle about to boil. He sounds dreamy. Who is he, Pat Boone's brother? Frank Sinatra's cousin? Rock Hudson's twin?"

Karen's luggage suddenly appeared before them on the conveyor belt. Allison wanted to leave before she blurted out more. "When I know more, I'll give you the entire lowdown. My next meeting with him is tomorrow afternoon. Maybe we can plan to talk about it afterward at dinner? I'll go pull my car up."

Before Karen could reply, Allison was out the glass doors on her way to the parking lots.

Within a few minutes, she had steered her car curbside, and they stowed Karen's luggage in the trunk. They drove away from the airport and were soon out on the main highway heading toward town.

"I'm a little tense about delving back into my job," Karen confessed. "Just being away for a week gave me a whole fresh perspective. It's not that I'm tired of the old routine; I love teaching photography, but it's just that I'm at a point in my life where I need to refresh some things."

Allison fully understood. "Breaking off an engagement can make you want to go in a new direction, and it's not unusual for that feeling to spill over to other areas of your life."

Karen frowned. "Like driving this old highway. We've been down this old road so many times I'm surprised there's not tire tracks leading straight to our apartment!"

"I can tell you're feeling a growing annoyance with the status quo," Allison said, hoping that if she showed extreme sensitivity to Karen's plight, her sister might not be too irritable when they returned to their apartment. "Maybe some music will help." She flipped on the radio. No sooner had she turned up the volume than her jaw dropped. She exclaimed, "That's him!"

Karen's head shot up and she glanced toward the sidewalk whizzing past them. "Where?"

Allison glanced at her watch. "On the radio! It's ten o'clock. That's my new client! He said his new song might be playing tonight!"

She turned up the volume a little more so they could both hear the record clearly. His up-tempo pop rendition of an old country song presented an entrancing, toe-tapping break from the conventional music popularized by Teresa Brewer, Nat Cole, and Tony Bennett.

"My goodness!" Karen finally cried out. "Be still my heart! That boy can sing!"

Allison nodded. "Yes, and he's as charming in person as he sounds. The big challenge he brought to me is how in the world we can capture that excitement in a photo or a press release. He's different from the others, and he needs something new, fresh, and different in his pictures. Who do we know who's talented with a camera and lights that might be able to capture his special appeal like no one else has?"

Karen and Allison exchanged weighty glances.

Karen instantly caught her sister's drift. "I'd love the job, Allison!" She sank back and let the music play havoc with her imagination. "He sounds familiar to me, somehow. Isn't it funny how some songs take you back to another time and place? For some reason, he makes me think of high school, but I can't place the voice. I'm sure I've never heard this band before." Suddenly, she gasped and sat bolt upright with an astonished expression. "Allison, he sounds just like . . . ."

Allison was surprised by her sister's abruptness. She took her eyes off the road and looked searchingly at Karen. "He sounds just like who?"

"Oh, it's so silly. For a second, when he said the word 'goodbye,' I thought he sounded just like a boy I used to know. Oh well. No matter. A new challenge is just the charge I need to prod me out of my doldrums!"

Chapter Six

The next morning at five o'clock, Allison heard her sister's alarm clock go off. This was far too early to get up, by Allison's standards. She did not generally rise until eight o'clock. One of the advantages of being self-employed was that she rarely scheduled an appointment before nine-thirty. Karen, on the other hand, had a stimulating job teaching photography at the Memphis College of Art. She had to arrive early enough to prepare materials for her eight o'clock class.

After Allison finally got up and dressed, she meandered into the kitchen. She was debating whether or not to have breakfast when she encountered the mess Karen had left behind in the sink—a bowl partially filled with pancake batter, a skillet on the stove filled with bacon grease, an orange juice glass, and coffee cup. *No wonder Karen has trouble with her weight!* Allison silently carped. *I don't feel like eating anything anyway, so I'll just skip breakfast and leave the dishes for her to clean up this afternoon. It'll be best to head directly for the committee meeting at ten. No doubt, they'll have coffee and danish there.*

She looked forward to attending industry meetings, especially when they were held at the Museum of Art in Overton Park, a 342-acre public park in Midtown Memphis that featured the Memphis Brooks Museum of Art, the Memphis Zoo, a nine-hole golf course as well as the Memphis College of Art, Rainbow Lake, Veterans Plaza, Greensward, and the Old Forest Arboretum. She could easily spend a lively morning or afternoon just strolling around the complex before attending a meeting, but not today. She was determined to stay focused on the business at hand, to concentrate on the issues to be discussed, and to brush from her mind her constant reflections about the young singer haunting her every thought. She was scheduled to meet with him later in the day, and if the previous encounter gave any indication, she fully expected to be bowled over by him again. This time, she vowed to skip the coffee and jelly donuts, and remain calm.

Allison sped down the freeway and veered onto the exit ramp that led her to the bustling downtown area. She chose a parking lot two blocks away, where rates were somewhat less expensive. She accepted a ticket from the attendant, and then hiked to the complex.

Ascending the stairs, she considered the people she would likely encounter: *Core people, undoubtedly*, she surmised. *The same people always come to these things. Now and then, a self-motivated newcomer shows up, but it would be nice to see new members. Just once, I'd like to leave one of these meetings feeling stimulated to the point of bursting!*

Today's meeting had been conveniently arranged. A conference room had been booked so attendees could easily walk to the nearby luncheon at the end of the meeting. Eight people were already deeply involved in a heated discussion when Allison entered. She looked at her watch and only then realized that she was twenty-five minutes late.

She hung up her coat, and as unobtrusively as possible, poured herself a cup of coffee. She ignored the picked over danish, then joined the others. Several people smiled or nodded as she slipped into a seat.

No sooner had the lively in-progress discussion concluded than a long-winded discourse on the Effective Use of Color on Paper Bag Advertising began. The dull subject soon left her numb because Blake, a balding, heavy-set advertising executive, merely droned on and on in a dreary monotone about the pros and cons of using red, blue, or yellow ink, and his speech was entirely devoid of any kind of audio visuals. Allison's thoughts quickly drifted to the young music sensation she had met. She had been so close to him that they could have been lovers at a drive-in movie. She was almost convinced that she had seen a sparkle of love light in his eyes, and that vision kept preoccupying her thoughts. When she tried to shake him off and study the printed program to discern if a more interesting speaker and topic would soon appear, she only saw him smiling back at her from the program. She clamped her hand down over his face so hard that the move embarrassingly jiggled everyone's water glasses. She finally resorted to tallying the thread count in her napkin, but even that task failed to take her mind off him!

She was deep in thought about what kind of portraits Karen might be able to take of him when she suddenly heard the moderator say, "Meeting adjourned!"

Before she could stand up, Blake maneuvered into the empty chair opposite her and cooed, "Allison, you should have come earlier. You missed all the latest gossip! Walk with me over to the luncheon—you *are* going to it, I hope—and I'll fill you in!"

Normally, she would have had nothing to do with Blake. Not only was she repulsed by his chunky build, shiny face, and protruding nose hairs, but his busybody approach left her more than annoyed. She looked at her watch. *I'll have to kill some time before the luncheon, and Blake can sometimes steer me toward new prospects if I can stand to endure his trite chit chat,* so she smiled and replied, "Of course. Let's walk over there together." Little did he know that she already planned to think only about her upcoming appointment with a man who was so exciting that he made all other men seem transparent. Blake would no doubt interpret her unusually serene and happy disposition as a sign that she was enjoying his company. Under the circumstances of having to tolerate Blake, her fantasies were finally a welcome diversion.

Blake waddled down the hall beside her, chuckling. He could not wait until they were out of earshot of the others to spill the beans about some news he had heard before the program meeting. "Oh, Allison," he beamed, "you know how competitive this business is. Even large agencies can loose well-established accounts. I've got to point someone out to you—someone who might have her eye on your client list and be thinking about stealing some of your business!"

As they entered the large hall, the place was buzzing with cocktail conversations, but his stingingly tart remark left her feeling uneasy. Blake took her coat.

"Thank you, Blake. What's this about stealing my clients?"

"I'll hang your coat up," he said. "See if you can find a strategic set of seats for us. I'll tell you after we sit."

Allison feigned confusion. "Oh Blake, I'm so sorry, but we should sit at our assigned tables." She walked away into the crowd, not really wanting to hear his gossip. Blake stood there disappointed that they would not be sitting together, but mostly puzzled that she had not been more interested in his hot scoop.

The hall was set up with a long podium at the front of the room that was lined with the keynote speaker, club officers, and prominent guests. Lavish green draperies had been drawn open to enable sunshine to fill the room. The day was so beautiful that Allison longed to be outside, but she dutifully found her seat. To her joy, she could sit between her friends, Jeff Unger and Marshall Wells.

As she gracefully maneuvered her knees beneath the yards of hanging table cloth, she playfully announced, "Why don't we abandon the meeting and go for a long walk?"

Jeff and Marshall laughed. They were media salesmen, working together for a company that sold space in national publications. They were always glib about their business, and Allison shared a positive-minded outlook with them.

The meal was typical for that kind of group affair. One had a choice of fruit salad or chicken. Allison chose the fruit salad, and she devoured the chunks ravenously.

"This is the first thing I've eaten all day!" she said.

"Slow down, girl!" Marshall affectionately teased. "You can have some of mine if there's not enough there."

Allison grinned sheepishly. "I *have* been inhaling this, haven't I?"

She dabbed her napkin at her lips, and suddenly noticed a dark-haired woman sitting at the next table who was staring at her. When their eyes met, the other woman did not avert her gaze. Allison felt somewhat unnerved and could not help but wonder if her hearty appetite and vigorous chewing had been offensive to the woman. She brushed her off, turned back to her friends, and asked, "Any new prospects on the horizon?"

Marshall began telling her about a new chain store, but Allison could only half listen. She nonchalantly glanced back at the dark-haired woman who was still intently staring at her.

When Marshall took a bite, Allison interjected in a whisper, "Please don't look at her too obviously, but I'd like to know who that woman is—the pretty one with the shoulder length dark hair and coal-gray eyes at the next table."

Jeff glanced surreptitiously at the woman, and then said, "That's Sharon Eaton. She's a media buyer. We worked with her once recently. She's one tough cookie. I'll say that much."

Marshall asked, "Why the sudden interest?"

"She's been staring at me."

"I think I know why."

"Why?"

"She's studying you. I heard before the meeting that she's expanding her agency—in direct competition with yours. I wouldn't be surprised if she doesn't already know your entire client list and she's plotting how to entice some of them over to her camp."

"How could she possibly know—"

Jeff interrupted quietly. "Word gets around. You know how that is. Everyone knows you've got some A-list local clients."

Allison was stunned to the quick. She could not eat another bite, gulped hard, and tried to disguise her rising anger by averting her eyes and playing with her napkin on her lap. An apple chunk had lodged in her throat, so she took a sip of water and shot another fleeting look at Sharon, but immediately averted her eyes again because the aggressive upstart was still gawking at her with a penetrating gaze.

Finally, Allison managed to clear her throat and softly ask, "How could that woman—and you, for that matter—possibly know details about my business? Is my office bugged?"

Jeff laughed. "Nothing as paranoid as that. Just industry gossip. Rumors in this town spread faster than fire. Be careful of her, Allison. You don't want to get involved with her. I'd keep my distance if I were you. She's surely heard that you've got a new client—what is his name? Elliot? Elden? Elwood? You know who I mean—the band singer you're trying to promote. I'm sure that Sharon knows all about him and she wants a piece of the pie!"

Chapter Seven

The keynote speaker began her introductory comments, but Allison scarcely heard a word the woman said. The shock of the news that Sharon Eaton—a hostile minion in the local advertising world, or a snake in the grass, as Allison was quick to peg her—was eyeing her client list to see whom she could steal left her feeling dizzy. Allison hid her emotions by feigning interest in the keynote speaker. She appeared to be looking attentively at the woman behind the lectern, but even though her voice was adequately amplified on the loudspeakers, Allison could not concentrate on her speech. Her mind simply reeled over that woman who was sitting at the next table.

At one point when the speaker cracked a joke and the entire audience laughed as one, Allison threw back her head with laughter in such a way that she was able to turn and look again in Sharon's direction. Sharon accidentally happened at that moment—or was she deliberately still eyeing Allison's every move?—to meet her glance with a smile. *Is she laughing at the speaker, or was she purposely smiling at me?* Allison quickly tried to gauge her gawking. The isolated moment was fleeting, because Allison did not let her smile linger. She looked back at the speaker as if she had not noticed Sharon at all.

When the luncheon was over, everyone split up into little cliques, but Jeff and Marshall could see by Allison's demeanor that she was visibly shaken. She was not her usual self, asking probing questions about their industry, working the room, and collecting business cards. Suddenly, she felt like a wolf had invaded her sheep fold. She stood shock still, appearing to be in the thick of things, but she kept a watchful eye on Sharon. At one point, Jeff asked her a question and Allison did not even answer, so wrapped up was she in monitoring Sharon's every move.

"Did you even hear me? Jeff asked.

Allison snapped back to attention. "I'm sorry—what did you say?"

"I asked if you like the agenda for next month's meeting. Allison, you seem upset. Are you stewing about Sharon?"

"Yes. I mean, no. Yes, I like the proposed agenda, but no, I'm not stewing about that woman. Don't worry about me. You should know by now that I can take care of myself."

"If it's an introduction you want . . . ." Jeff looked from her to Marshall, ". . . it's an introduction you'll get! I already know that she wants to meet you, but you need to remind yourself that if Sharon Eaton's interested in you, she's got a reason. And when Sharon has a reason, you're best off keeping her at arms length."

"What is she, a leprous ogre?"

Before Jeff could reply, several people came up to Allison to comment how interesting the speaker had been. She acted like she had been absorbed in the entire speech and savored every moment, but in fact, she merely wanted to get away from the place, and she did not want to meet Sharon . . . not yet. She said a quick goodbye to Marshall and Jeff, and left with a book tucked under her arm that had been given out to the first hundred attendees. Her mind was on other matters. *Why did this Sharon Eaton want to meet me? Why were Jeff and Marshall so brutal when they talked about Sharon? How will my meeting this afternoon turn out? There's so much to tell Karen later. Where will I start?*

She was halfway across the lobby and almost to the coat rack when she heard Marshall calling out, "Allison! Wait!"

She turned to look back and was astonished to see Marshall with Sharon in tow—or was Sharon taking the lead and practically dragging Marshall to initiate an introduction to her? She appeared to want to meet Allison, but she seemed more like a blood-sucking octopus in a newfound garden of fresh tropical fish, and she was wasting no time in heading toward her.

Allison watched as they made a beeline across the lobby toward her, and then Jeff suddenly burst through a side door from the meeting room and practically ran to catch up with the three of them.

"Jeffrey!" Sharon greeted him warmly and extended her arm so they could shake hands. "How good to see you! It's been too long since our paths crossed!"

Allison noted the strained expression that passed across her friend's face. She knew that Jeff did not like to be called by his formal name, but somehow, when Sharon said the name, the sound was so natural, so intimate. *Had Jeff had some sort of liaison with this woman which embittered him so? Jeff and Marshall had said she would go to any lengths to get what she wanted. What had she done to entrap them?*

Jeff kissed Sharon on the cheek, a kiss that was similarly returned in kind. He casually slipped his arm around her. *How hypocritical we all are at times,* Allison mused. *I wonder, does she think as highly of him as he does of her? Or is it simply this advertising business that makes us behave in a two-faced way at times? They'll be over here in another moment. Why not stay put and force Sharon to paddle across the entire length of the lobby to meet me? At least I can meet her from a position of strength!*

Allison planted herself firmly, like a Grecian statue connected to the core of the earth, and radiated an expression of gentile curiosity that neatly covered up her outright disbelief at the woman and her unmitigated gall. The two men were smiling at the impending introduction as if the moment was a Prelude to War. Allison stood firm, but she held out one hand as if to invite them nearer, even though Sharon was heading in her direction like a torpedo launched from a submarine.

They were still six feet apart when Marshall practically shouted, "Allison, I want you to meet a friend, Sharon Eaton. She's as capable a media person as you're likely to meet in this town. Sharon, this is Allison Webster. She's in the creative end of things. I thought you two might want to meet."

Allison studied the woman who stood in front of her, taking a quick mental picture of her that burned into the retina of her mind. *While she might very well be capable in her work, the adjective Marshall selected to describe her would have been the last one I would have used in an introduction.*

Before her stood a beautiful woman. She was not more than five-foot four and weighed, perhaps, ninety-five pounds. Sharon had fine facial features that were framed by her feathered, dark wavy hair. The suit she wore drew attention to her tiny waist and accented the curves of her body. *Surely any man in the room would be delighted with the opportunity to spend time in this woman's company,* Allison assumed with a slight twinge of jealousy.

Sharon smiled widely. Allison noted the deep colored lipstick she had expertly applied in a way to accent her large white amazingly straight teeth. *Caps!* Allison was quick to conclude. *Her eyes sparkle with self-assuredness, and she's wearing a lot of expertly applied makeup. I can smell her delicious perfume. She knows just how to use Fifth Avenue's latest offerings to her best advantage!*

Sharon spoke with exuberance. "So you're Allison Webster. I've heard so much about you and your work. What a pleasure to finally meet!"

Allison wondered, *What—if anything—have you heard about me . . . and from whom have you heard it?*

As if to answer her unspoken questions, Sharon continued her praise. "Marshall and Jeff recommend your services all the time. You certainly have admirers in these two. Funny that we've never met up until now!" Sharon smiled again as if to give Allison her cue to speak.

What's funny about that? Allison asked herself. *You've dropped into my world with the suddenness of a cruise missile!* But she responded out loud, "Yes, isn't it? I guess we've clearly been working with different clients."

"We *have* been."

"Perhaps that will change," Allison suggested in a voice that smacked of a heroine in a Harlequin romance. "Who knows what the future may hold?"

"Don't you?" Sharon's expression had turned hard. She smiled now, but the smile had no warmth. "I'm glad we had the chance to meet here. I'd love to stay and talk, but I have an appointment with Phil Samuels that was scheduled weeks ago. No point in being late!"

Do you think I don't have a busy schedule, too? It was you who waylaid me while I was on my way out! "It was nice to meet you. Hope to see you again soon."

"Oh, you will!" Sharon said, as she shook Allison's hand.

"Have a good day."

Sharon scampered off like the White Rabbit in *Alice in Wonderland*.

"What a strange introduction!" Allison commented. "It certainly didn't last very long."

"Long enough to establish a relationship," Jeff replied.

"A relationship? I felt like Melanie Wilkes meeting Mata Hari!"

Jeff chortled and shook his head. "They're from different eras."

"You know what I mean!"

"I told you Sharon was up to something."

Marshall joined in. "She's so pretty. You've got to admit that. Sharon has those perfect china doll sort of looks."

"And a china doll sort of stiffness, too," Jeff remarked.

"Don't let her looks fool you," Marshall warned. It's only skin deep. She's lethal. The lady has no conscience."

Allison pulled her coat from the rack. "How old do you think she is, Jeff?"

Jeff helped Allison with her coat. "About thirty-two, thirty-three, I'd guess."

"She's never been married," Marshall commented.

"Well, I'm not married either," Allison said. "That doesn't mean anything. Anyone as attractive as she could get any man she wanted. She's obviously a career woman with strong ambitions. She said she had an appointment with Phillip Samuels. Who is he?"

"He's the owner of Star Records," Marshall said.

"Oh?"

"I'd guess that she's muscling in on your efforts," Marshall put in. "She must want your account bad. Why else would she be running to see him?"

Allison tried to hide her true worries. "Maybe she's planning to shoot her way into the lobby and take the company by force? Perhaps she's been watching too many John Wayne movies and thinks a hand grenade works better than a handshake? In any case, why should I be worried? What's Star Records or Phillip Samuels got to do with me?"

"That's the record label that just put out your new singer's record."

Chapter Eight

Allison had failed to clarify that little detail about Star Records earlier. The revelation came to her like a hammer blow. She returned to her office emotionally exhausted from the psychological brow beating she suffered during her momentary confrontation with Sharon Eaton. The advertising vulture was said to be on a quest to devour clients belonging to others.

Allison looked at the clock over Marge's desk. The time was a minute to three. As if her secretary read her thoughts, Marge said, "You've got an hour until your next appointment."

"Thank you, Marge. I think I'll have some afternoon tea," Allison mused out loud. "I need to pull together some ideas for him."

"Before you do, you need to read this message he left for you. He called hours ago to ask if you wouldn't mind meeting him at the Arcade diner on Main Street. He left his number."

Allison studied the clock again. "The Arcade? I've barely got time to gather my things and drive there. He must have a tight schedule today, or maybe he was on business in the vicinity and thought he'd be late arriving all the way over here. Of course I'll meet him at the Arcade. Would you be kind enough to call him and let him know? I'll just grab my things now and be on my way."

"Sure, Allison. Oh, by the way—he said he'd be wearing blue suede shoes."

"Blue suede shoes?"

Marge shrugged her shoulders. "I stopped trying to second guess you young folk a long time ago. I couldn't imagine what men could possibly like about a dumb blonde like Marilyn Monroe, and look what happened!"

•

Allison nearly flew from her office to her apartment just so she could change clothes. The Arcade was no fancy restaurant, but the diner was popular and usually crowded. Sometimes, patrons had to wait more than an hour just to get a seat in one of the lumpy booths. They did not go there for the ambiance but for the nationally famous food and occasionally famous customers. The restaurant had become known as a place to see and to be seen.

Allison changed into a silk lilac-colored shift that was tightly cinched at the waist. Its long full sleeves gave just the right amount of extra color without being overly dressy. She carried her paperwork in a smart leather folder, and a nearly-matching purse accessorized the ensemble without giving her too much to carry. She did not want to lug a briefcase and look like a lawyer preparing for trial. After a final moment of scrutiny in front of her full-length mirror, she locked the apartment door and dashed down the hall.

As she reached the elevator, she pressed the button and waited. The elevator was between floors, but coming up. When the doors opened, she ran right into Karen, who emerged clutching her large portfolio case.

"And where are you going all dolled up?" Karen demanded to know. "I thought you and I were having dinner together. I've been waiting to hear all the news you were going to share with me!"

Allison smiled slyly. "It'll have to wait."

"Who is he?"

"I've got an extremely important early dinner engagement."

"So I see. And I repeat: who is he?" She eyed her sister's outfit and nodded to show her approval. "I'm sure he expects you'll add some spice to the meal—or should I say the evening?"

"Karen! You're always assuming there's more to these situations than there could ever be. This is a business meeting. If I thought the way you do about such matters, I'd be—"

"You'd be having a lot more fun. Relax. I'm sorry if I've gotten you worked up. I want everything to go well. You look lovely. You're very capable, and you've got lots of talent. Go get 'em!" Karen turned and headed for their apartment.

Allison emerged from her building to the parking lot. *This afternoon—and maybe tonight—will be important. I don't want to get my hopes up too high, but I'm finding that suppressing my excitement is too difficult. An early dinner with any handsome man at the Arcade is an adventure, but with him I can't help but believe that something wondrous might happen!*

Allison found that keeping her mind on the road proved difficult. She wondered, *What could he be wearing with blue suede shoes? How many people will be inside the diner? Will any of them be famous? I met Patti Page there once, so you never know who might show up. So what if there's no candlelight and flowers? There's more to enjoying a man than being distracted by such superfluous things like that. Besides, I already know enough about him to know that just being with him is going to be great. And those booths are so sweet! You can either sit side by side or sit across from each other, lean forward, and look into each other's eyes without a thought about anyone else in the world. I wonder if he's thinking the same thing right now about me? Could he be?*

That thought was tantalizing and almost too much so. She bit her lip just pondering the possibility. As she turned the corner onto South Main in the downtown area, she tried with little success to snap back to reality. *This is, after all, just a business meeting,* she cautioned herself. She drew in a deep breath in an effort to calm down. Still, she could not stop her heart from racing in anticipation, as she drove to the intersection at Patterson Street and saw the bright neon sign arched over the restaurant's front entrance.

The restaurant was packed. The bright atmosphere and the din of dozens of conversations going on at once seemed almost overwhelming. Allison looked for her date, but all she saw was the crowd of people occupying all the booths and boomerang tables that were faded and worn around the edges due to thousands of coffee cups, plates, and elbows rubbing across them.

The seating hostess noticed her searching gaze and asked, "Can I help you?"

"I'm meeting someone. He might be here already. You might have noticed him. He's probably wearing blue suede shoes. I wouldn't be surprised if he's—"

"Right here," a soft baritone male voice said from behind her.

Allison turned to see him standing so near to her shoulder that she could not help but smell a whiff of his Sportsman Aftershave. She felt his warm hand touch her shoulder. He said, "I sure am glad you could come here on short notice. You look like a million dollars!"

Allison laughed. "Thank you! Do you still have to make a reservation for a simple booth here?"

"Everyone does," he said. "I eat here so often they should name a booth after me."

The hostess said, "Let me show you to the booth!"

They followed her down the aisle. Allison looked ahead to the farthest booth that he seemed to prefer. She had to think fast about whether to slip into the seat that backed up to a wall, or to take the seat facing the wall. *If I sit with my back to the wall, he'll be facing me and can look only at me and there'll be few distractions while we talk about his work and what I might do to help, but if I let him take that seat, I'll be able to see only him.* In a snap decision, she slipped into the back seat so that he would see only her. *That'll be better all the way around!*

No sooner were they both seated than an overly-excited teenage girl wearing a tight red angora sweater ran up to their table clutching a 45-rpm copy of his latest record. "I know you're him!" she gushed, pointing to the name on the record. "Can I get your autograph?"

Before he could answer, she thrust him a pen and her record. He graciously laid the record on the table and signed his name on the dust sleeve, and when his head tilted down, a long curled lock of his hair fell becomingly over his forehead. He seemed to not notice, and when he smiled at the girl and gave her back the record, she was so overjoyed she actually curtseyed before running off.

Allison was instantly overwhelmed. Now that she could finally relax, she was still in knots. He was just as desirable as she remembered, but she recalled that he was also as unattainable as before—if not more so. She asked, "Does that happen often?"

"Not so much yet. Our first record just came out, but it's happening more and more."

"It would be nice if some of your future records featured your picture on the dust sleeve along with some space for you to sign an autograph when asked."

"That would be good, which is another reason to get some great new pictures. I was on Dewey Phillips' radio show a few days ago. Listeners were phoning in wanting to know who I was. A lot of them think I'm a colored guy."

"I'm sure that a great photographer could get some wonderful shots of you that would clarify that nicely. In fact, if you ever make a whole album, the cover ought to have your name in great big letters superimposed over a live concert photo of you singing and playing your guitar. I have a good photographer in mind already!"

"I don't have much money, Allison."

Allison addressed his remark. "When we position you right to maximize your potential appeal with the girls, I don't have any doubt that the nickels and dimes will come rolling in. The key is to show you in just the right light. Girls like the one that was here a moment ago spend every night thinking about their dream guy. Record albums are like paper dolls to them. They also cut out pictures from all the popular magazines, tack them to their bedroom walls, and dream, dream, dream."

"Just like guys?"

"The same. Don't you have any sisters?"

"No, I'm an only child."

"Well, I'm sure your mother had her favorites, just like all women and girls. Who knows? You could end up in the movies like Marlon Brando and James Dean! But it all starts at the beginning. Having a winning portfolio is one of the first steps. I'd like to arrange a sitting with a talented photographer as soon as possible. We can work out payment details later. I think the photographer I have in mind will do them as a favor to me."

A waitress came up to their table. "You ready to order?"

"I haven't even looked at the menu!" Allison exclaimed.

"Your date's been here before," she said with a wink at him. "I bet he knows what he wants."

He replied, "The best thing they have here is a fried peanut butter and banana sandwich."

Allison was amused and shocked. She laughed and said, "Are you kidding? A fried peanut butter and banana sandwich?"

"You never had one?"

"No, but I'll try it!"

He said to the waitress, "Bring two. And a big glass of milk for both of us."

He smiled warmly at her. Allison's eyes met his, and she was glad that he had his back to the restaurant so he could see only her. He held her gaze affectionately, and neither of them batted an eye, which was especially difficult for Allison because there was an awkward congestion taking place in the aisle just behind him that he could not see. Their waitress had to sidestep a group of three large men surrounding a dark-haired woman trying to push their way down the aisle at the same time four people from another table were trying to leave. The hostess had difficulty steering the arriving group toward the empty booth across the aisle and practically at Allison's elbow, but as soon as the aisle cleared, the foursome noisily slid into the booth. Once the three men were out of the way, Allison saw the woman for the first time at the same moment she saw Allison.

"Miss Webster!" Sharon Eaton exclaimed with a smile. "Imagine the two of us running into each other twice on the very same day!"

Chapter Nine

Allison's jaw dropped. Sharon Eaton was the last person she wished to see. She looked stunning in a smart sleeveless dress that revealed slightly sloping lily-white shoulders. Her dark hair was pulled back and on top of her head with stray curls that fell down her neck in a studied yet alluring way. Allison regained her composure quickly enough to smile back, hoping that her shock had gone unnoticed. She tried to smile, but she instantly perceived that the evening would most certainly not turn out as she hoped, not with Sharon sitting across from them eavesdropping on every word they said. Her companion was completely oblivious to the invasion of their privacy, but Allison could not have been more perturbed if a television camera and a microphone had been shoved in her face.

Sharon grinned triumphantly, like a spider with a victim in her web, and then she launched into a quiet monologue, while her male companions sat in stony silence.

Allison remembered, *Marshall warned me at lunch that Sharon didn't mind stepping on anyone or anything in order to get where she wanted to go, and that she always got what she wanted. Is she deliberately here to antagonize and spy on me?*

When Allison's companion began sweetly telling her about his mother, she tried to look attentive, but his words melted in her ears into something akin to the soft strums of a guitar. She could not focus clearly on him while having to continually glance back at Sharon, who she was certain was hanging on his every word. She noted the same hardness in her face that she had become aware of earlier that day. *Could it be that she's as tough as Marshall and Jeff said, or does she somehow feel threatened by my obvious bond to a client she craves? Oh, that's just tomfoolery! I'm sorry for her! She's in for a rude awakening! There's no way I'm going to let her lasso my new client away from me, or any of my other clients, for that matter! They all love me and are 100 percent satisfied with my work! I'm not going to lose this client in front of me!*

Suddenly, he completely distracted her by taking her hands into his. She felt the warmth of his flesh and felt slightly tickled by the rough calluses on his fingertips, no doubt the result of years of holding down guitar strings against a fret.

He said, "You might think that because I travel a lot, there's a girl in every town. But there's not. Being close to you like this makes me feel like I can trust you."

If the entire world had suddenly crumbled around them, obliterated everyone else, and left them alone and exposed only to God, the sun, and the sky, Allison could not have been more astonished. "Oh, you can!" she managed to say.

"I feel like I can talk to you. Together, we can take all this in a new direction, someplace where even I've never been before."

Allison tried to comprehend what he was trying to say, but then Sharon suddenly screamed across the aisle in a voice so loud that an air raid siren would have had trouble competing with her. "Why Allison, what a coincidence this is!"

The blast of her verbal intrusion thundered across the aisle like a steam roller trying to flatten Allison. The tone in her voice seemed galling, but Allison tried to deny the nonverbal cues that beamed through so clearly: she had completely leaned over the man sitting beside her and was practically shouting at her in a volume that utterly obliterated even the clatter of plates and the din of other voices in the restaurant. All the while, she twirled one curl around her finger, flirting with Allison's poise.

Allison shot a glance at her date. She sensed that he, too, was somehow irritated by Sharon's remark, since they had already been interrupted once by the teenage girl accosting him the very moment they had taken their seats. Allison thought, *If she doesn't lighten up and mind her own business, the impending consequences will be more than unpleasant!*

Sharon either failed to pick up on the negative vibes rising from Allison like smoke from a volcano, or she deliberately chose to antagonize her further by continuing her boorishly intrusive harangue. The man sitting beside her leaned back even more so Sharon could bend forward a few additional inches, as if shoving her mouth closer to them with the force of sledgehammer blows would endear her to them. "I was just telling Phil Samuels this afternoon that his artists would benefit from some masterful public relations guidance. What with the growing popularity of television, the profusion of magazines, plus the tie-in with teen-themed movies that are so trendy in movie theaters and drive-ins, the national audience for his artist's records is unlimited!"

Sharon's face took on the expression of a tennis player lobbing a victorious serve, but Allison looked like Winston Churchill hearing that the Germans were advancing across the sea toward England. Her hands were still held warmly in his, which under other circumstances might have been the first step toward completely losing her heart to him. However, under Sharon's penetrating, microscopic gaze, his simple, normal show of affection that would have been the thrill of the night suddenly made her feel extremely exposed and uncomfortable. She prayed that he would release his grasp, and was relieved when he did so. She suddenly realized that he had no idea in the world who the brazenly forward, rudely aggressive, loud-mouth shrew across the aisle was, nor why the blatantly antagonistic person, who had suddenly taken on a strong resemblance to the Creature from the Black Lagoon, was upsetting the genial atmosphere of the diner and turning the setting into a podium from which she could broadcast her perception of industry trends.

Sharon then had the cheeky audacity to bypass Allison as if she was invisible and ask the man she was obviously on a date with, "Aren't you the hot new singer billed as 'The Memphis Music Man?'"

"Yes ma'm," he said, "sometimes. I guess we haven't met. I worked with Mr. Samuels on a couple of recordings. You're probably right about what you said, but Allison here is already on it!" The warmth in his voice would have seduced her into believing that there was more tenderness behind his speech than the words indicated. In one fell swoop, he acknowledged Sharon genially, yet sprang to Allison's defense by turning the tables and confirming that she was the one he had chosen for professional assistance. Allison felt her angst lifting as if a hundred pound weight was being removed from her back.

Sharon, however, was quick to pick up on that and modify his meaning with more comments. She interjected in a decidedly business tone, "I'm sure, and yet still, there's so much to attend to!"

Allison had enough and spoke up. "And I can't think of a more marvelous place to conduct business than the quiet, intimate atmosphere of my office. Let's make an appointment to meet one day."

Fortunately, the waitress appeared from out of nowhere, so Allison could not see Sharon's reaction. The waitress balanced two plates on one arm and two large cold glasses of milk in her other palm. She expertly slid the plates on their table and managed to set the two glasses down without spilling a drop. Best of all, she completely blocked Sharon's view of them. "Those sandwiches look great!" she said. "And look at him, he's beaming from ear to ear!"

She was right. He was broadly smiling and looking straight into Allison's eyes. "Since it's your first, tell me how you like it," he said, leaning back and waiting for her response. He was a man who did not care to impress others by dropping names, dates, and places. He wanted to know if Allison liked the unusual meal that she was experiencing for the first time in her life, not if she was going to put on a floor show for the benefit of the uncouth, monopolistic business burglar across the aisle.

Allison could see he wanted her to like his selection, and so she raised one half of the sandwich to her lips. While she did not know anything about the subtle art of creating fried peanut butter and banana cuisine, she wanted to give her sandwich more than the cursory consideration she generally would have. She sniffed the sandwich and said, "Lovely aroma!" as if she was savoring the bouquet of a wine.

They were both concentrating so fully on Allison that when she parted her lips to take her first bite, they parted theirs in unison with anticipation of her reaction.

Allison took a ladylike bite and then sat back to take pleasure in the taste. "Ah, this is very nice!"

The waitress was somewhat more interested in pleasing men, Allison could tell, but in a motherly sort of way. She was obviously entranced by the man in front of her, but not in a predatory way like Sharon. "See? He's smiling again! You made a good selection for your date, young man!"

His smile showed off his large, pearly-white teeth, and the waitress grinned and squared her shoulders triumphantly. For some unknown reason, Allison realized that the moment was important to him and that he sincerely wanted for her to appreciate his choice.

The waitress also acted as if the entire restaurant's reputation hinged on Allison's verdict. "I'm glad you like it, honey!" she crowed, and then swished away, proudly satisfied.

"Very nice? Just very nice?" Sharon suddenly shrieked, as soon as the way was clear. She now had a direct shot at Allison again, and she screeched in a tone that faked amusement as a thin disguise for ridicule. She proceeded to lobby a volley of questions at her as if she was an interrogation officer for the German Gestapo. Allison was sure she saw her tongue fork like a serpent. "My dear, don't you know what you're eating? The Arcade's menu has earned them an international reputation! Everyone in Memphis and across all fifty states has heard of their award-winning signature entrée! You've lived here for years and you're just now trying one? Where have you been hiding, in a hole somewhere?"

Sharon came across with all the charm of a vulture in an Edgar Allen Poe story, and she made Allison feel embarrassed. Allison thought that perhaps she ought to have been more effusive in her praise of the sandwich, but the peanut butter delightfully stuck to the roof of her mouth, and she could not politely launch into a long-winded tirade like a restaurant critic in *The New Yorker* espousing the pros and cons of the flavor, aroma, and texture without sounding like an ill-mannered lout.

Fortunately, her companion rallied to her defense. "I think she's a charmer! I like a girl who hasn't been around and tried everything. That she likes it is good enough for me. Maybe she'll be brave enough to try a Tutti Fruit fizz next time!"

Allison took a big gulp of milk to wash down the sandwich, and then she cleared her throat. She was finding that keeping her words to herself was proving to be difficult, yet reacting to Sharon's colossally rude outburst had become necessary. *Remember, you're with a client, whether he has more than a professional opinion of you or not. Don't let her drag you into a caustic shouting match here in this public setting, not with one of the nicest men*

I've ever met sitting only a few inches across the table from me!

"Actually, I really find I like southern dishes more and more, the more I travel," Allison commented, if only to get Sharon's goat, even though she instantly realized that her choice of words had been awkward, to say the least. She stopped just short of giving in to an uncontrollable urge to hurl her plate at her like an Olympic discus thrower. Reining in her vengeful impulses, she merely replied, "This sandwich is nice, but I do hope we can eat the rest of our meal without any further interruptions. Would you mind letting us talk in private?" She smiled at the entire foursome, including the men, who were sitting like stone images while Sharon mocked her, but Allison did not wait for Sharon to answer.

Allison worried that she had made a fool of herself. As if to confirm her suspicions, Sharon began to snicker, and that was the last straw. Allison felt the blood rush to her neck and face. When she began to experience heat radiating from her cheeks, she knew that she had achieved that deep shade of crimson that told all. She wished now that she had not said so much. *A sufficient response would have been to simply compliment him on his selection and leave it at that. Why didn't I do that? Instead, I think I did a masterful job of expressing precisely the wrong sentiment at a clearly critical moment!*

Allison could not have been more wrong. "Thanks for getting us some peace," he said. "If you don't mind, let's just talk to each other for a while no matter who else tries to interrupt. No point in leaving because of the crowd. If you're half as hungry as me, beating this place will only make us hungrier. Enjoy your sandwich. While we eat, I'll tell you about some of the songs we're going to do next."

He took a big bite of his sandwich, and Allison finally had time to collect her thoughts. He was doing his best to see that she was comfortable. In his company, she managed to forget the earlier sequence of events. His smooth manner all but obliterated the memory of Sharon, who could have given the Wicked Witch of the West a run for her money.

"How about love songs?" Allison asked. "Love is probably the one thing girls think about most often." She took another bite and looked deeply into his eyes.

"We're looking for songs about stuff like teddy bears, a girl wearing a boy's ring around her neck . . . and love in every way that comes around. What we want to do is hit some kind of a nerve with young people like us, who want to break away from our parent's way of doing things, forget about the war once and for all, and be different."

Allison was impressed that he had tried to establish a heart to heart relationship with her. She was about to take another bite, when he set his napkin down and pushed his empty plate away. She saw his lip again curl up slightly at the side as he smiled. "I'm counting on you to help us do it, Allison. You're the best!"

Evidently, he appreciated her. As much as she wanted him to express much more, she was content for the moment to have his true approval. "Thank you! I'll do my best!" she replied sweetly, while grabbing the opportunity to demurely bat her eyelashes once at him. She allowed her chest to swell with pride, which drew attention to her perfectly shaped bosom. Her actions were not lost on him.

"I know I'm in good hands."

"As a matter of fact," Allison added with confidence, "my little sister's a very talented photographer. I think she'll love taking some fashionable shots of you."

"That's convenient keeping the business in the family. But you better tell your little sister to be careful and not do what her big sister's done."

"What's that?"

"Make me fall for her."

Chapter Ten

Whipping wind in Allison's hair brought just the effect she had hoped. She practically floor-boarded the gas pedal on her convertible and finally was able to feel herself breathe more freely. Best of all, Sharon was out of her face. Meeting her twice in one day left Allison feeling drained. *Being near that woman even for fleeting moments is like facing Dracula. In fact, Sharon has all the attributes of a blood-sucking vampire hell bent on draining the lifeblood from others!* The gust of exhaust Allison left behind obliterated the scene in her rear view mirror. She also sensed tension slowly leaving her body with the realization that a wonderful guy had finally come along that thought she was more than just a professional whiz-bang. Now she knew how Scarlet O'Hara felt in *Gone with the Wind,* when Ashley Wilkes admitted that he loved her.

Hearing kind words from a man she knew hundreds of other girls adored left her feeling rejuvenated. That meeting had confirmed the fact that she would indeed be doing promotional work for him. She was committed to doing a fine job for him. She wanted him to be pleased. *Or is it that I want to please him?* she dared to ponder.

A short while later, Allison walked briskly down the hall to her apartment. She was trying hard to dismiss the hot and bothered feeling Sharon had caused that she could not shake. When she opened the door, she was greeted by the television blaring in front of Karen, who was draped in her terry cloth bathrobe and reclining on the couch.

Allison snapped, "Do you have to play it so loud?"

Karen's response was to turn the set off, and then she replied sarcastically, "I can see things went well for you this evening! What happened, did his guitar string snap and pop you on your keester?"

"I'm sorry. I didn't think you'd be up this late, and I was craving some peace and quiet."

"Are you kidding? I'm sorry if you didn't get the job. There'll be lots of others. You've just got to—"

"I've got the job! He needs me!" Allison looked jealously at Karen. Deep down inside, she knew that Karen would never let herself get so worked up about a man that she had only recently met, nor would she be as upset as Sharon had made her. Allison felt tears misting in her eyes.

Karen noticed. "Allison, what's the matter?"

"I'm such a jerk! How could I ever have imagined that meeting the most wonderful man in the world wouldn't be offset by being crushed by the most horrible female on earth?"

"Wait a second. Wait a second. There are some scenes missing from this story. I know about your new client, but who's this Bride of Frankenstein that made you cry?"

"Sharon Eaton." Allison bit off the words as if she was announcing Adolph Hitler. "She's a conniving threat to me and every other marketing executive in this city. She reminds me of that girl in *All About Eve* that plotted and schemed to take over Bette Davis' life and career."

"I know Sharon."

Allison was taken aback. "You *know* her?"

Karen answered matter-of-factly, "Uh huh. She moved her office here from Nashville about a month ago. We shot some pictures for one of her clients."

Allison was stunned to the quick. "She's that new? Well, that explains why I hadn't heard of her before. I was introduced to her today at the monthly ad luncheon, and then ran into her again later at the Arcade, or I should say was assaulted by her there."

"She's a leech!" Karen interjected. "She's got a reputation for undercutting others and sometimes seducing her way into getting a stranglehold on clients. Who's she trying to steal from you?"

"Why would you say that?"

"Because that's what she does best. She's not tops at providing what her clients need most, so she tends to lose them after six months, but she has no equal when it comes to gaining new accounts. Her trouble seems to be keeping accounts for the long haul. That's probably why she moved from Nashville. She exhausted the pool of prospects to the point where she had no alternative but to look for fresh blood, like a vampire. Is she going after your accounts?"

Now, Allison could see the big picture more clearly. "She's probably trying to horn her way into the Memphis music scene, slithering up to Phillip Samuels and hoping that she can get first crack at all the upcoming recording artists that pass through his studio. But I think I've got the best one of the bunch! And there's more to my bond with him than just a business deal!"

"You haven't shared all this with me yet. What a wonderful opportunity! What a fantastic account!"

"It's astounding, isn't it?" Allison felt her mood swing into more positive territory. Her sister often had that effect on her. "I'm not excited simply because there's got to be work in it for me—and you—but he's just the most simple and down to earth guy I've ever met. Why just today, he taught me how to enjoy a fried peanut butter and banana sandwich!"

Karen grinned from ear to ear. "That really does sound serious. Marriage usually follows."

Allison grinned. "Most of all, he needs new, carefully styled photos. That's where you come in. We're going to think of just the right imagery, and you're going to get the poses on film. We're going to have a lot of fun with this, and who knows—maybe something more will develop besides a set of 8x10 glossies!"

"That reminds me . . . you haven't shown me a picture of him."

"I don't have any, except for a grainy one-inch black and white halftone I clipped from the newspaper, and that one looks amateurish! That's why he needs us."

The two women sat and excitedly discussed the work that they would be doing shortly. They felt like they were lost in a dream, flipping through all the movie fan magazines and making notes about what poses and what kind of lighting effects captured the best qualities of the male stars. Rarely did they get the opportunity to work on such a coveted account as a star in the making. They both realized that the new campaign was a trial of sorts. If all went well, they were both assured of more work from him, and the more deeply they brainstormed, the more they began to realize that if they played their cards right, maybe they could inherit the trust of Phillip Samuels and become the backbone of his company's efforts to market new music talent to the burgeoning teenage market.

"Can you imagine anything more fun than styling photo and promotional campaigns for all the handsome young men singers coming through Memphis?" Allison asked rhetorically, knowing that the question hardly required an answer. "I must say it would be a welcome change from working on industrial safety garments and grocery chains!"

Both Allison and Karen laughed. Allison continued, "I think there'll be quite a bit of work for you to do, Karen. I know I'll need to use a lot of photographs, but I also want to have wonderfully romantic illustrations in the ads. They'll capture the fantasy—the dream boy—every girl wants to have in love with her. And who better to fulfill those fantasies than a handsome young man in his twenties with a great big head of gorgeous hair and a voice that can make a girl swoon—a devil in disguise as the angel Gabriel? Who knows? We may graduate to working with the big Hollywood stars! Can you imagine? What if that fourteen-year-old "irrepressible Ricky Nelson" grows up into a gorgeous heartthrob who can sing? Or Paul Peterson from *The Donna Reed Show*? Or Johnny Crawford from *Rifleman*? We might end up working with them all!"

Karen felt the need to put a damper on her sister's discourse. "Hold on, Allison! It's one-thirty in the morning, and you've already got the two of us heading up MGM! How about a good night's sleep before we have to get ready for our close-ups?"

"Don't you want to know about what I've got planned for us?"

Karen stood up and yawned. "Sure I want to know, but I've got to get up much earlier than you. Being the Queen of Hollywood will have to wait. Besides, Cecil B. DeMille may not yet be ready to abdicate his throne!"

"You're right, of course. I guess I've let my enthusiasm get the better of me. Still, we've got our first assignment, and everything begins with a dream, doesn't it?"

Karen yawned again. "That's what Dr. Frankenstein said. Look what happened to him." She trudged sleepily to her room and shut the door most of the way, but then opened it and peeked out. "I think your new man's going to be good for you, Allison. And when he sings, he sounds like Dean Martin, Little Richard, and Pat Boone all rolled into one, plus a little something extra . . . that special something that makes him unique. He might also be thinking the same thing about you!" She winked and closed the door for good.

Allison folded up the magazines and tidied up the living room before going to her room. *I don't want to think about him any more tonight. But she's right. He does have that special something. I'm going crazy over him after having only just met him a day ago! On the other hand, this sudden turn of events has spun my life into a more complicated and confusing merry-go-round than it was before. At least I know where I stand with him. I just hope that working so closely with him won't push him away from me!*

Suddenly, the telephone beside their sofa rang and Allison's head shot up. *Who could be calling this time of night? A wrong number or a crank call?* She picked up the receiver.

"Allison?" The deep voice she already knew so intimately sounded even more sublime when he said her name. She felt as if he had just strummed every string in her heart.

"Oh! Hello!"

"I'm sorry to call you so late. I just wanted to tell you how much I liked having supper with you today. I found your number in the phone book. Have you looked out your window?"

Allison was confused. "No, I've been working with my sister all evening on some ideas for you. I only just now decided to go to bed."

"Look out your window. There's something I want you to see."

Allison was puzzled over what in the world could possibly be outside her window that he knew about and wanted her to see. Fortunately, the cord on her telephone was long enough to stretch the entire width of the room. She parted the blinds and looked outside. "I don't see anything."

"Sure you do. Look up."

"There's nothing but the moon."

Allison could not believe her ears. The next thing she heard was him strumming his guitar and softly singing just for her the upbeat, blues-flavored song about a blue moon—his new record—the one all the local radios were playing every hour on the hour for teenagers, but she was hearing the real, heartfelt solo version that no one else in the entire world would ever get to hear. Allison cherished the moment that was so special, so personal, and more transcendent than if her blue moon had turned to gold again.

Chapter Eleven

Allison floated through the following morning on Cloud 9. Never in her life had she felt so alive, exhilarated, and desired, like Jane Wyman in the romantic movie *Magnificent Obsession*, when Rock Hudson said to her, "Once you find the way, you'll be bound. It'll obsess you. But believe me, it'll be a magnificent obsession."

Allison and Karen had tabbed the object of her magnificent obsession for his first photo shoot the following day. Karen had booked a small portrait studio for the occasion, but she was ill at ease over the fact that she had never actually met him. She wanted to first experience the full impact of him in performance so she could capture the essence of his charm on film. To fully comprehend him, she and Allison journeyed to see him that night in an appearance at the Overton Park Shell.

The Shell held court as one of Memphis' most popular concert venues, an outdoor open-air amphitheater surrounded by a huge green park, where concertgoers could sit in chairs or spread out on blankets under the stars. When Allison and Karen arrived about a half hour before the show, they were astounded at the turnout. Country singer Jimmy Rogers headlined the show that day, and a few other acts were scheduled to follow him, including Allison's magnificent obsession in the third slot. However, more than 500 other girls arrived who also harbored fabulous fixations on him. The wooden fence surrounding The Shell quickly became as useless as a strip of paper. Crowds pushed against the fence, sat on the top rail, and climbed over to gain free admittance. The mob became too great for the scant security patrol to do anything to halt the tidal wave of teenagers. Karen and Allison were forced to take seats near the back, and they were lucky to find seats at all.

Everyone sat patiently through poor Jimmy's set, giving the singer a polite round of applause, but by the time he finished, the concert promoters were keenly aware that the fans were impatiently ready to storm the stage in their mania to hear the hot new singing sensation scheduled to follow Jimmy. The promoter wisely moved him ahead into the second slot.

The audience was not disappointed. He strolled onstage to thunderous applause, wearing wide-cut sequined pants that emphasized his movements when he nervously sang and shook one leg. His glitzy attire was a powerful gimmick that had brought Liberace much success in his shows, and a sensational attention-grabber for wrestler Gorgeous George. The stage device worked equally well on young music goers.

"I was hoping to get a good look at him," Karen whispered, "but from this distance, he resembles a hairy jumping bean in sequins!"

"He's really a lot more handsome up close," Allison replied.

"I hope so. Photographing jumping beans isn't my specialty, you know, unless you land a Mexican food account. In that case, we'll talk."

The band immediately launched into his second song and young women screamed throughout. At one point, he abruptly launched into a slow, grinding tempo that was accentuated with energetic, exaggerated body gyrations. The crowd went even wilder, and the band's drummer egged them on by underscoring his movements with bump and grind drum licks that he had mastered while playing in strip clubs. The kids may not have fully understood exactly what was driving them into a frenzy, but the drummer certainly did. The stunning effect on the audience was unprecedented.

While the young people felt as if they were in paradise, some staid adults felt as if the gates of Hell had opened and the Devil was at the microphone, especially when he took over the piano during one song and began pounding frenetic chords eight to the bar.

If his act had concluded with him being shot from a cannon, some adults viewing the show could not have been more shocked. One old man standing next to Allison turned red with outrage. He said to her, "That kid is a danger to this country! He's stirring them up like—you know—it's vulgar!"

Other adults nearby blushed and also chimed in:
"This is disgusting!"
"It's animalistic!"
"This isn't a family show; it's burlesque!"
"That music belongs in a bordello!"
One appalled woman asked Allison, "Would you want your family to see this?"

Allison pointed to Karen and said, "My sister *is* here."

Karen grinned, lightly waved, and winked at the woman, who gasped in shock and then stormed off in a huff.

The next morning, the *Memphis Daily Appeal* carried a full report of the phenomenon that had taken place the previous night, complete with lurid news photos of what they termed an "out-of-this-world musical pin-up boy" that had electrified the audience. Across the city, various pastors sharpened their pens to denounce the brazen boy in fiery sermons from their pulpits that upcoming Sunday.

None of them know that a shy, idealistic, and tender youth devoted to his mom and dad lurks beneath his flamboyant stage act! He's only in his early twenties, and sure, he possesses the red-blooded passions any healthy young man would have, but he's as gentle as a teddy bear, a big hunk of love, who only wants to find the girl of his dreams. And that girl is me!

Although she did not wear his promise ring, and in fact, had not received a single gift from him, she thought nothing of the matter because she had only just met him days before. *It's too soon for me to expect any gifts from him,* she reasoned. *Besides, I can't step away from the fact that I'm here because I was recommended to him by a client because of my ability to help businesses succeed. His business just happens to be music—and exciting girls—but that doesn't change a thing! Karen and I are professionals, and no matter what we might deeply feel about a client, we're obligated to keep a level head about things and prove our professional worth.* She had nearly convinced herself that her business sense would overrule her emotions, but then she could not help picturing in her mind what her new monogrammed towels might look like someday if his last name became hers.

The hour for their first photo shoot arrived the next day. Allison made certain that the studio was clean and neat. She found an electric coffee pot and supplies and started a pot to boil. While she waited, she thought about her outfit. She had wanted to create a somewhat avant-garde if not bohemian impression for their first photo shoot. She wore a loose fitting, smock-like top that was made of a colorful material resembling an artist's palette at the end of a painting session. The smock crowned a pair of tight fitting, severely tapered Capri pants. Then, she had added high heels for a finishing touch.

Karen did not want to show up early for fear that would make her appear too anxious. Allison had a half hour to kill. She went to the employee lounge and surveyed the soft drinks in the vending machine. While searching the selection, she could not help but see her reflection in the glass. The smock made her look shorter than she had hoped. She chose a root beer and sat at one of the tables sipping her soda, waiting for half an hour to pass. Two girls from another office came in, and Allison could not help overhearing them chatting about the concert that had taken place at The Shell the day before.

"Wasn't the show just divine? What a sweetie!" a short, plump secretary said. "How many people do you think were actually there?"

"Five or six hundred, I'd guess," her all but anorexic companion replied in-between cracking her gum. "I just think he's the most wonderful doll! He's single, right?"

"Foot loose and fancy free, that one is. If he's got a girl, no one knows about it. Frankly, I don't expect he's going to settle down for some time. You know how musicians are."

"So who's talking about settling down? I'd love to sink my hands into that lovely, thick mass of hair . . . ." the short, plump secretary fantasized, ". . . and he's so sexy!"

Allison glanced up at a large wall clock near the entrance. She had heard enough. Hearing them discuss the guy she was attached to left her feeling somewhat annoyed, even though they were discussing his stage character, not him in real life. Besides, she had only fifteen minutes until he was expected to arrive. She got up and returned to the studio.

No sooner was the coffee ready than Karen arrived in a whirlwind. She burst through the door clutching a bundle of camera bags and notes that made her resemble a frenzied shopper at a clearance sale. She took one look at the outfit Allison had selected and said, "Who are you supposed to be, Madame Toulouse Lautrec?"

Allison's heart sank and she bit her lip. "It makes me look short, doesn't it?"

"Well, let's just say that if that smock was any lower, you'd be sweeping the studio floor when you walk. The overnight cleaning lady will probably thank you!"

Allison sighed and began fiddling with the fabric. "Maybe I can knot the front so it looks more Greenwich Village?"

"Never mind the smock. We're not in Greenwich, we're in downtown Memphis, and we've only got a few minutes to get the studio set up before your Mr. Wonderful arrives.

While ideas are still fresh in my head, why don't you scurry around and set up some light stands and a tripod and unroll some backgrounds? And is that fresh coffee I smell brewing?"

"Yes. Over there. Help yourself. According to our layouts, a sky-blue background will accent the golden glints in his hair. I'll start with that one."

"That's a good choice," Karen said, as she unloaded her supplies. "Why weren't you thinking that clearly when you were in your closet this morning?"

Allison knelt and began unfurling a large blue paper roll. "Now you're going to make me feel embarrassed about what I'm wearing! I thought this would give me a sort of artistic, free-wheeling look."

Karen headed for the coffee pot. "It's free-wheeling, alright. A Dior model couldn't roll it down a runway if she tried."

The studio receptionist suddenly stuck her head in the door. "Are either one of you named Allison?"

"That's me," Allison replied.

"I'm just the hired help," Karen told her, as she poured a cup of coffee.

"There's a delivery man with something for you."

Allison said, "Tell him to bring it in."

"He left it here outside the door. You'll have to come and get it yourself."

The girl abruptly disappeared. Allison struggled to her feet, brushed off her hands, and went to the door. When she opened it, she gasped and screamed.

Chapter Twelve

Someone behind the door was holding a cute teddy bear up like a puppet. Allison heard him say, "Run your fingers through my hair and cuddle me real tight!"

Karen appeared behind her and curiously glanced over her shoulder. "Hmm. A talking teddy bear. Either your new client is Edgar Bergen, or we've got a big problem!"

The man said, "I'm the guy the newspapers call an "out-of-this-world musical pin-up boy." Is it safe for me to come in?"

When he suddenly showed his face, Allison burst out laughing, but Karen merely dropped her jaw. She was speechless and took a step backward, nearly spilling her coffee.

"You're right on time, as usual," Allison said, as she opened the door fully. She looked perplexed at Karen. "You'll have to excuse my sister, Karen. Usually, too much coffee makes her talk too much, so I'm not sure why she suddenly looks so flabbergasted."

"That's because she didn't expect to see *me*!" he said, entering. "How are you, Karen? It's been a while!"

Karen struggled to regain her composure. "I'm—I'm fine!"

"It's always fun running into an old girlfriend. When Allison told me about her sister, Karen, I never thought she meant you!"

Now, a look of unadulterated shock spread over Allison's face, while Karen took a turn at being pleasantly surprised. Had an atomic bomb just gone off, Allison could not have been more astonished. In a split second—not unlike the bomb that exploded Hiroshima—the word "girlfriend" ricocheted through her ears into her head, down to her heart, and then back up to her brain, where it gonged more loudly than the bells in Reims Cathedral on a Paris Sunday morning.

Before she could rationalize the full impact of their surprising disclosure that just detonated in her face, Allison instantly melted. The object of her affections extended the teddy bear to her as an obvious token of his adoration. His gesture was sweet and overwhelming, especially when blended with his mind-boggling confession and her realization that he and her sister had been engaged in some kind of a recent romance. He had obviously dressed with care in a long-sleeve, red and blue striped shirt that showed off his deeply tanned, handsome facial features, and he wore his hair stylishly cut and combed high up and back from his face. His entrance and profession of affection for Karen simultaneously left Allison feeling both deeply disturbed and rapturously enthralled.

Karen giggled, "Would you like some coffee? Allison was kidding a moment ago. I've only had a single cup."

"Sure! Thanks!"

"Allison?"

Allison felt as if she had just been bowled over by a speeding truck. She could only stammer, "Y—yes. You *know* each other?"

Karen replied flirtatiously, "Know each other! We were voted the 'Couple Most Likely to Get Married' at our prom!"

Allison wanted to say something, but could not find the words. She simply stood there with a fake smile on her face while staring at the two of them.

He broke the awkward silence by holding out to her the teddy bear again, saying, "I'd like to be loved like your teddy bear. When I'm away from you, maybe this will do instead."

Allison took the charmingly lovable gift and held the toy close to her heart. "That's so sweet of you. Thank you!"

He reached around to the outside of the door and retrieved a garment bag, while Karen said, "You don't know how many times I've thought of looking you up again. After all this time, I guess it was just too tough summoning up the courage."

"Oh, come on, Karen," he pleaded. "Make this easy for both of us." He put his arms around her and embraced her. She hugged him back.

As she headed back to the coffee pot, she teased, "Now this was a dirty trick. Here I was half expecting to have to impress some world-weary traveling musician, and *you* show up!"

"Instead, you got a guy who already knows you like coffee with sugar and heavy cream, so why are you drinking yours black."

She poured him a cup. "Allison and I aren't on home team turf today. We've invaded someone else's studio, and they don't have our usual coffee supplies."

He turned to Allison and noted, "You're sure quiet all of a sudden."

"I'm sorry," she replied. "I so anticipated your arrival this morning that I'm still stunned that the two of you know each other."

Karen handed him his coffee, and he said, "Thanks. Your sister hasn't changed much."

"Well," Karen replied, "it's only been a few years, but you've certainly changed!"

"No, only my circumstances have."

"I know! When did you start performing? You never showed any inclination when I knew you! We saw you yesterday, but I didn't know it was you. You were terrific! I'm amazed!"

"Karen," Allison interjected, "how was it that the two of you met? Where was I when all this was taking place?"

Karen poured coffee for Allison. "You were away at Vanderbilt, studying all the time. I was a high school senior, and we were in love. I told you about him."

"I don't think you did."

"I did, but you were too preoccupied to think much about it." She handed Allison her coffee and thought back to their torrid romance. "I was sure that he was the only man I'd ever *really* love. We almost got married."

"I thought it was now or never," he added.

"But there were complications. Our parents all objected on the basis that we were too young to commit ourselves, and being young and impressionable, we buckled under to the pressure. Then, I moved away, but many times, I wished that I hadn't listened to Mother!"

"It's alright. Only fools rush in. You had no way of knowing you were going to see me again this morning."

"And Allison," Karen noted, "could think of nothing but you. Right now, I'm afraid she looks like a hurt puppy dog!"

Deep inside, Allison could have cried at that moment, but she wanted to make sure she played her cards right. She was still madly attracted to him. She raised her coffee cup to her lips, using the moment to cast her eyes downward to the brew so they could not see into her misty eyes, and she said, "I'm just excited to have the chance to do some good work today, that's all. I guess I'm a little overwhelmed to discover that you knew each other intimately."

Karen looked at him, and he grinned widely. Suddenly, they both burst out laughing!

"The most intimate we got," he said, "was when she fell asleep beside the pool one day and I took an ink pen and connected the tiny moles on her back!"

Karen said, "Who would have known they formed the Liberty Bell? You see, Allison, it was a high school romance. Nothing more."

"We spent a lot of time together in our senior year," he said, "but malt shops, movies, and going to the local hangouts with our friends was as far as either of us dared to go. And since you're both here now, I suppose I can control my animal instincts. Just keep me away from ink pens!"

"Perhaps it's time to change the subject," Karen suggested. "Since we're renting the studio by the hour, what do you both say we get down to work?"

He sighed. "I'm as ready as I can be this time of the morning."

"Allison, show him the sketches you made."

Allison was only too glad to refocus their energies on something productive. Being broadsided and knocked senseless by this mind-boggling revelation left her numb. Working on her campaign ideas shifted their talk to a more even playing field, where she could sidestep the unpleasant upset of learning that her sister had earlier ensnared the boy of her dreams. *According to them,* she explained to herself, *their love was nothing but a high school romance that, like the stars at morning, soon faded away. I trust Karen. She's always been up front and honest with me, especially about boys. And I could already tell, over the last two days, that he's someone I can take at face value. I'm the one who wears her heart on her sleeve, and I've got to be careful not to act like a jealous schoolgirl. At this critical moment, I should just be myself, the Allison he's come to know, appreciate, and adore. Nothing less will do!*

Allison made her presentation effortlessly. She flipped through the pictures that she had previously selected and confidently laid them out for him to inspect, showing just exactly how careful poses, when lit properly and shot with a high quality camera and lens, would show him off to his best advantage.

He was immediately enamored with her work and said with admiration, "These are great! Leave it to you two to put your fingers on exactly what I need to do."

Allison glowed and said, "I certainly appreciate your compliments!"

"Oh poo!" Karen said. "He's astute enough to know what works and what doesn't. If we remember the impact his looks and style had on the audience yesterday, we can safely say that we're not the only creative people in Memphis. I know my way around a camera, and Allison knows how to craft a campaign as good as or better than Madison Avenue. We'll pool our talents and come up with something great!"

They soon had the photo flood lights on full blast. Allison cut the ceiling lights from a switch by the front door, and Karen began taking a variety of poses of him in front of the blue background. The most striking were some extremely close facial shots that had him looking dreamily into the lens as if he was looking right into a girl's heart.

"These are looking so good!" Karen exclaimed. "Why don't you go put on one of the other outfits you brought?"

"Sure thing!"

He had no sooner retreated to the back than the front studio door burst open and in walked Sharon Eaton! Allison looked up and her jaw dropped. Sharon blithely tossed her coat aside and dramatically entered with all the subtlety of the Allies landing on the beaches of Normandy. She exclaimed, "Darlings! What a quaint, little arrangement. You've done such an adorable job with the decor. Did you do it yourself? I know you did. Who else would dream of using a stark minimalist décor to create the illusion of a big city professional studio!" Without asking, she rudely flipped on the overhead lights at the switch by the front door.

Karen doused the floodlights, while Allison could barely hide the fact that she was appalled at Sharon's rude interruption. Nevertheless, she managed to stammer, "What are you doing here?"

Sharon feigned confusion. "I belong here!"

"This is a private session."

"Not any more. I joined the Board of Directors at Star Records, and I'm looking forward to seeing how our new boy on the block—our #1 talent—goes through his first promotional shoot for a national campaign! Don't worry, kids, I'll take over from here and make sure that I get him on a fast track to success!"

Chapter Thirteen

Allison resented Sharon's high and mighty air, but she was not about to lower herself to Sharon's standard and snap at her. For the second time that morning, she had been nearly bowled over by unexpected revelations, the latest of which was Sharon's boast that she had somehow wormed her way into Phillip Samuel's good graces. *No doubt*, she figured, *for the sole purpose of attaching her tentacles to every single artist that comes near the place!*

"How nice of you to drop by," she managed to say in an even tone, despite the fact that she was already red-faced with barely suppressed rage over Sharon's interference and invasion tactic.

Sharon began rifling through her purse for something. "Oh, I wouldn't have missed this for anything. There's a lot at stake. We've got so much to discuss and clarify!"

Karen drew near and interjected. "I didn't realize we were going to be working together. Although we don't mind you being present, we're in the middle of an intense, private session, and I'm afraid you've somewhat broken the mood. Would you mind taking a seat on the far side of the studio so I can continue?"

Thank you, Karen! Allison thought. She could barely suppress her joy over her sister's comment. *Karen's always perceptive of my feelings, and she no doubt sensed that I was put out at Sharon for invading the confidentiality of our work.*

Sharon fished a crumpled pack of cigarettes from her purse and began plucking at one with the tips of her long red talon-like fingernails. "Do I know you from somewhere?"

Karen answered tersely, "We've never met, but your office hired me to shoot the Anderson account photos last month."

Sharon lit her cigarette and exhaled two long plumes through her nostrils that momentarily made her resemble a medieval dragon. "Oh yes, I remember. We managed to find a couple of shots from the session that were somewhat usable. I'm sure you're finding this handsome young singer a more interesting subject, aren't you?"

Karen could not hide her icy tone. "I enjoy working on all types of accounts, Miss Eaton."

Sharon seemed oblivious to the fact that there were no ashtrays in the studio and that the management had placed a non-smoking sign up to announce their policy due to the presence of dangerously flammable photo developing chemicals. She practically ordered Allison, "Do find me something I can put the ashes in, dear."

Reluctantly, Allison wondered, *What can I find that will do? We don't have any hand grenades!*

Sharon flounced into a leather chair, crossed her legs, and announced, "I have some bold ideas for this campaign. Tell me what the two of you had in mind so I can determine if your ideas will work. I don't want you to deviate from the direction I want him to go."

The sharp, cutting edge of her comment made Allison dread whatever was next in store. She had already learned from her two awful confrontations with her that the two of them were as different as sandpaper and silk. As she fished around in a waste basket to retrieve a used paper cup for her to use as a makeshift ash tray, she thought *I don't like her! Still, I've worked with other people I didn't care for in the past. I just hope I can hide my feelings this time and hopefully bite my tongue!*

As she set the cup on the coffee table in front of Sharon, Karen again rallied to her defense. "We've done a thorough analysis of his needs and understand the styles driving the popularity of his band's music. I think I'm managing to capture the essence of his appeal quite nicely."

Sharon responded somewhat crassly, "I hope you're doing better than you did with those other photos. We could only use two from the entire session! I just started to brainstorm on some ideas to present to him this morning that might be more appropriate than what the two of you came up with."

"Oh? I guess you're not the eager beaver I figured you to be. Allison already has detailed a fabulous campaign with images carefully designed to enhance his fan appeal. I already know that Allison has her finger on the very attributes that he most wishes to convey to his fans, and I'm safe in saying that if you attempt to stray too far from those ideals, Star Records might lose him as an artist. I shouldn't have to remind you that regardless of his contract with them, the band is ultimately responsible for themselves. You haven't signed an artist management agreement with him, have you?"

Sharon blew a puff of smoke purposefully in Allison's direction and she ignored Karen's question, choosing instead to turn the tables on her. She sneered, "Have *you* signed a contract with them?"

Allison was incredulous over what she was hearing. "We have an agreement, probably not as special as one that I'm sure you've already got planned! Now listen here, I don't know what you mean to achieve, but I know where I stand!"

Sharon looked at her with an expression of amusement, as if she was watching Shirley Temple throw a tantrum. She inhaled a deep, lung-filling drag on her cigarette and then practically belched the fumes again toward Allison. "Phil Samuels and I have known each other for a long time. Why shouldn't I have something special planned for his rising new star?"

Allison nearly choked from the smoke. Her eyes began to water and she felt intimidated by Sharon's gutsy demeanor. She now realized by Sharon's comments that she and Phil had probably been heavily involved in some way or another, an idea as unsavory as Sharon's disgusting smoking habit.

Sharon added, "What Phil and I have is of primary importance to me. It's taken me a long time to cultivate our relationship. I don't want anyone coming along and spoiling it, Allison Webster. In fact, I won't *let* anyone spoil our plans!"

Allison struggled to keep her composure in the face of Sharon's total lack of delicacy. She retaliated, "I have no plans to disrupt your relationships, personal or otherwise. As far as I'm concerned, Phillip Samuel's just another president of another company. I'm doing work for an artist, who may or may not have a long-term relationship with Phillip Samuels. Do I need to remind you of Star Records' reputation? So far, they're a small fish in a big sea. I believe this artist may go all the way to the top, in which case, I'd look for him to advance to a bigger label with the money and clout to market his work to the largest audience possible. In the meantime, we have every intention of going forward with our efforts to prepare him for the success he deserves."

Sharon flicked her cigarette at the cup and missed, dropping ashes in a fiery clump on the floor and ignoring the dangerous mess. "I need someone who's on board with our team. You seem to harbor some kind of resentment, despite the fact that you don't have any contract with him. A verbal agreement isn't worth the paper it's written on! *We* have an iron-clad contract. If we decide to sell that contract to a larger label, that'll be our prerogative. I'll be involved in any negotiations to that end, so you might as well get used to the idea that I'm part of the picture, here, now, and forever after. I'm so glad we've been able to clear the air so quickly. We should be able to work well together . . . so long as we understand each other."

"You mean as long as I don't get in your way?"

Sharon smiled at Allison's verbal dart, withdrew some papers from her purse, and laid them on the coffee table. She then voiced her next statement with extreme care. "As long as you cooperate, Miss Webster. I've brought a copy of the list of publications I'm getting information on that I expect he'll be interested in appearing in. You'll be wise to fashion your layouts according to their standards of acceptability."

"How thorough you are," Allison said. "I'll appreciate knowing, too, which magazines you're inclined to select as you come closer to those decisions. It will help me refine my proposals." No sooner had she made that comment than she thought, *I wish I could retract that! It sounds like I'm dying to be of service to her, which isn't the impression I meant to give. She's got me so nervous, and with him in the back changing clothes just out of earshot! I've got to sharpen my wits if I'm to duel with this woman. She comes charging in here uninvited, plows over Karen and me like a steamroller, and then expects me to bow to her like a buttercup in the breeze!*

Sharon dropped her cigarette in the cup, where it laid smoldering and befouling the air. She gathered up her purse and began walking to the door while talking over her shoulder and out of the side of her mouth. "I'll let you know. Let's stay in touch. Help me keep Phil happy. We'll be planning to announce the fall lineup of new releases at a huge media gathering at the Peabody Hotel. We've reserved the entire indoor pool as a setting for a formal, glittering VIP party. I'll be wearing a new diamond-studded gown by Coco Chanel! We'll send you an invitation."

She turned the knob and was about to leave, but stopped and looked back. "By the way, don't be seen in public with our Wonder Boy anymore. I don't want his reputation sullied."

With that cryptic slur on Allison's character, she flipped off the overhead lights at the switch by the front door, and left. Since the photo flood lights were already doused, Allison and Karen were plunged into near darkness. Tobacco stench lingered like a pall over the entire studio, and a heavy cloud of smoke hung in the air like a shroud. Allison began fanning the air, stomped out the glowing ash embers piled on the floor, and ranted, "Oh! That woman! I wouldn't be surprised to find out that she was Mussolini's personal assistant ten years ago! I don't know if I can stand to be around her another moment!"

"Well," Karen began, "look at it this way . . . Mussolini was shot and hung upside down for the entire world to see. As for Sharon Eaton, we can only hope! At the very least, maybe she'll fall into the Peabody swimming pool while she's posing in her diamond-studded Chanel gown!"

Allison pictured that for a moment and then burst out laughing, and Karen joined her. They were doubled over chuckling, when Karen asked, "Do you think 'Wonder Boy' overheard any of that?"

At that moment, the back door opened and he emerged wearing his striking stage attire. He took one look at the two of them huddled together in the dark beneath a cloud of smoke and said, "I've heard of mood lighting and smoke pot effects, but isn't this going a little too far?"

Chapter Fourteen

Allison and Karen's photo shoot with "Wonder Boy," as Sharon Eaton brazenly referred to him, went off without a hitch after Sharon had slithered from the studio. When she was gone, Allison was glad. She had thought she would enjoy working on her new account. Now, she questioned that assumption. *It all depends on how often I have to interact with Sharon Eaton!* she decided.

The show must go on, and "Wonder Boy" departed to get ready for another outdoor concert. Karen stayed behind to develop her pictures of him, and Allison retreated to the comparative sanctity of her private office.

The next day, Allison found herself virtually alone in her office building where Saturdays were always quiet. The peace and solitude gave her time to concentrate on specific details in her proposals. She worked diligently, but found her thoughts wandering. *How could Karen have managed to be so fortunate to have known him before me? That was an incredible bit of coincidence. Thankfully, their passion cooled during the time they were apart, but still, I'd be a lot more comfortable with him if I had him all to myself!*

The morning passed quickly. Allison did not mind studying the list of magazines Sharon had unceremoniously dumped upon her to review, and she was professionally curious to gauge whether they would do the band any good. She took time to uncover their strengths and find a way to integrate them into the overall creative plan, more to help him than to appease Sharon.

Outside, a rumble of thunder caught her attention. She gazed from her desk to the sky, which had turned into a softly churning sheet of gray while she had been engrossed in the details of her work. Since bad weather had not been in the forecast, she had not brought an umbrella, and she had dressed somewhat carelessly in a comfortable pair of washed-out blue jeans, a baggy sweat shirt from college days, and sneakers. She had avoided applying makeup, knowing that not even Marge would be in the office, much less any clients, but going outside and getting wet was not in her plans. When rain began to patter against her window, she was glad she had thought to grab a banana and an apple for lunch and toss them in her purse.

She had just peeled her banana when she heard a knock on her office door. *Who could that be? Karen would call before driving all the way over here.* She rose to go to the door, but stopped first to survey her reflection in the glass on a large picture adorning her wall. She shook her head in disbelief. *I wouldn't have dressed this way if I had known someone might be coming in to see me. I don't like the idea of being alone in a deserted building with someone at the door!*

The knock came again, louder this time.

There was certainly no way to avoid the unwelcome intruder. She took a big bite of the banana to fortify her courage, and went up to the door and asked, "Who's there?"

A virile, masculine voice replied, "Special delivery. I have a special delivery for Miss Allison Webster."

How peculiar! Allison thought. *Is someone playing another practical joke?* She stood paralyzed with indecision, but then she called out, "Please leave it by the door. Someone will get it later."

"Special delivery. I need a signature."

She took a deep breath and opened the door. A startling guitar strum sounded, and then she heard *his voice* singing the whole first stanza of his new hit record. He moved out from behind the door and continued singing.

"You sound just like some guy on the radio!" Allison coyly cried with delight, gladly opening the door wide enough for her new boyfriend to come in without banging the guitar neck on the door.

He continued singing as he entered, and Allison followed him into the office, but when she passed the picture on the wall, she saw her dreadful reflection again and nearly died. There she was holding a half-eaten banana with the peels dangling over her hand, her hair pulled back in a stringy slipshod knot, with her baggy sweatshirt making her look like a member of an overweight exercise group.

He, on the other hand, had dressed with care. He would have looked wonderful to her even if he had not sported a rich tan that was visible beneath a tight white short-sleeve knit shirt. He finished singing and smiled his most winning smile.

Allison said, "What a surprise! How did you know I was here?"

"I called your apartment, and Karen answered. She said you were working today."

"Aren't you supposed to be getting ready for an outdoor concert?"

He set his guitar down. "The promoter cancelled the show on account of the rain. It's good to see you! I couldn't keep my mind off you all morning! Why are you working on a Saturday?"

"I put the finishing touches on the campaign I've drawn up. Would you like to see it?"

He laughed. "Are you kidding? I came to kidnap you. I'm here to have a good time, and I want you to have a good time with me. We can have a lot of fun today."

"In the rain?"

"The rain'll stop, but the concert will still be cancelled. I've got the whole rest of the day off, and so do you."

"Well, thank you, but I have some other tentative plans."

"Yeah, I know about those. Karen told me you two were thinking of doing something together this afternoon, and I suggested she make other plans because I wanted to take you out. She said that was fine. Now, we'll be able to spend the day alone—just you and me."

He bent his head down toward her head and firmly placed his lips on her lips. She could have tried to stop him, but she did not wish to. His kiss was gentle but strong so that she could not help but respond. She ached inside to be his and momentarily blocked out everything else. He pulled her close, and she heard him almost inaudibly groan with the pleasure of her body next to his. "Oh Allison, Allison, Allison," he whispered to her, enjoying the sound of her name as it danced across his tongue. He kissed her again, this time more passionately than before so that she knew she must succumb to her desire for him. "It's so wonderful to be here with you like this for the first time. And you know I like the taste of banana!"

He was kind enough to allow her to somewhat pull away so she could fully regain her composure. "Maybe I could freshen up a bit before we go?"

He chuckled. "I guess I did catch you off guard, didn't I? I couldn't be sure what frame of mind you'd be in if I popped in on you, but I'm glad you're willing to be with me. The rain's already slacking up. We can do all kinds of things this afternoon!"

Without any firm plans where they would go, he whisked her by her apartment so she could change clothes and gather a few things. Then they drove through the crisp, rain-scented fresh air to a Dairy Queen, where they picked up some sandwiches for lunch. The next stop was Memphis Central Station, where he deposited his car outside the depot.

When he gave her his hand to assist her from the car, Allison once again felt the electricity she experienced every time he touched her. She resigned herself to the fact that she would probably always react this way and must make every effort not to divulge the fact that her mind reeled.

Once they started walking up to the depot, he did not let go of her hand. He held the food sack in his left hand and gently caressed her other hand. He remarked with the enthusiasm of a young boy, "I always enjoy coming here. Maybe it's because I liked riding a train with my parents when I was a kid. It's still fun!"

Once they entered the bustling depot, he bought two round-trip tickets from Memphis, Tennessee to West Memphis, Arkansas, which was only about an eight-mile excursion. They boarded the *Golden State*, a six-year-old full-fledged streamliner that boasted smooth-sided cars with a paint scheme of vermilion red on the upper body and natural corrugated stainless steel on the lower body. Heavyweight baggage cars, dormitory cars, a dining car, and an elevated observation car were also attached.

In minutes, the train resumed operation. The observation car quickly filled with other visitors so that the two of them were obliged to sit extremely close to one another, like lovers in the front seat of a car at a drive-in movie. With a rumble and a roar, the train began to roll, and in only minutes, they were crossing the Frisco Bridge that spanned the Mississippi River. A few minutes later, they reached the West Memphis train station. From the station, they road in a quaint two-seat horse-drawn cart to the East Broadway Historic District, where they strolled along Beale Street West, passing music and nightlife venues that were more than equal those in Memphis, and they window shopped at a few of the cute little stores dotting the sidewalk.

"I'm glad you're here with me," he confided.

"Me, too," she said sincerely.

Suddenly, he squeezed her hand and said, "Don't look now, but here comes a photographer."

From out of nowhere, a photographer hopped in front of them. They both politely smiled and posed, and then she asked, "Are you selling pictures? Can we buy a copy?"

"I don't sell these. I work for the *Memphis Daily Appeal*."

"The newspaper?"

"Don't be surprised if this picture's in tomorrow's edition."

He disappeared as suddenly as he had jumped in front of them. Allison did not mind the extra attention, but she suddenly recalled Sharon Eaton's icy edict that she not be seen in public with "Wonder Boy."

"This happens to me more and more lately," he said.

"I'm surprised you take the matter so casually," Allison remarked. "I'd be on pins and needles if I knew there was a newspaper photographer around every corner!"

For a fleeting moment, she envisioned receiving a terse telephone call from the bossy, meddling Star Records Board Member admonishing her for daring to "sully his reputation" by appearing in public with him, but she quickly dismissed the annoying notion. *I won't have Sharon Eaton dictating what I can and cannot do in my private life,* she vowed. She was again distracted all of a sudden when he asked, "How are you on bumper cars?"

"Bumper cars?"

"They're everyone's favorite at the amusement park on Mud Island. One of the picnic tables there would be a good place for us to eat our lunch!"

Allison had nearly forgotten that he carried their lunch bag, and since she was too overjoyed at the way the entire afternoon was playing out, she heartily agreed by replying capriciously, "Of course!"

They hopped a passing taxi that sped them down I40 to the river walk, where they boarded an old-fashioned Riverboat that took them across the wide Mississippi to Mud Island.

"Time's a wasting!" he declared. "Let's head over to the picnic area!"

Hand in hand, the two of them playfully ran across the lawn to a perfect table positioned under the spreading boughs of a Poplar tree. Just like when they dined at the Arcade, she had barely touched her sandwich when he had finished and leaned on one elbow, happily satisfied.

He gazed at her adoringly and admitted, "I could take a nap right here on the grass, but maybe a spin on the bumper cars will perk me up again. What do you think?"

Allison had never been one to greatly enjoy being bruised, bumped, and battered by Kamikaze vehicles careening around and wildly slamming into each other, but she wanted to seem agreeable since he was so obviously keen on the idea. As soon as she could manage to swallow enough to respond, she smiled and congenially said, "Oh that would be fun!"

The next few minutes passed all too quickly, and they were soon in line to board the infamous ride along with a throng of other adults and kids. The attendant watched until everyone was safely in their vehicles—their last moment of safety, Allison feared—and then he cranked up the music on the loudspeaker.

"They're playing your record!" she called to him. "Maybe we can—"

With no warning, the electric current turned on and all the vehicles suddenly lurched forward with sparks splintering off the rods that shot upward from the cars to the metallic ceiling.

Allison glanced fearfully at the overly anxious kids hunched over their steering wheels, and before she could gather her bearings, someone immediately slammed pell mell into her from behind, snapping her neck back with whiplash and knocking her vehicle into an out of control spin that left her turned the wrong way on the course. He roared with laughter and sped by her, but a bevy of other kids pointed the noses of their vehicles in her direction, too, and they bore down upon her with the intent to ram. She screamed, but too late. One particularly powerful vehicle driven by a kid with the face of a gargoyle collided with her at such force that she was knocked backwards and rear-ended another vehicle. Then, two other crazed drivers crashed into her from both sides, nearly crushing her like an accordion into her steering wheel and practically throwing her from the car. By the time the three-minute ride was over, she felt as if she had been beaten and battered.

"Wasn't that great?" he roared with relish.

Allison was counting her bones, but she said, "Oh yeah! Real fun!"

Fortunately, she recovered once they were back on solid ground and strolling through the serenity of the botanical gardens. After that, night fell, and they returned to the Memphis and Arkansas Bridge. Walking across, he stopped her mid-stream. For a moment, they leaned on the rail and just took in the inspiring view of the great Mississippi winding into the horizon with the Memphis skyline draped in subtle hues of orange and gold. They were silhouetted against the sinking sun when he kissed her. He held her close, and for what felt like a glorious eternity, he refused to let her go. Cars may have been whizzing by them, but she saw nothing other than the tender look in his eyes, and she heard nothing except the passionate breath that passed between the two of them. Those heavenly moments created a perfect end to a nearly perfect day.

Time seemed to stand still, as they meandered hand in hand along the walkway over the slow-moving river. By the time they reached the far end of the bridge and took a taxi back to the train station, the first edition of the morning paper had come out hot off the press. He bought a copy from a paperboy as they were boarding the train back to Memphis, and sure to his prediction, the entertainment news section featured their picture in a 3-column by 5-inch space with a coy caption that recalled a phrase from his popular song, "Memphis' Music Man with Mystery Mama. That's Alright, Mama!"

Tomorrow, the whole city will know that we're an 'item,' Allison thought worriedly.

As if he was reading her mind, he said, "Tomorrow, everyone will know that you're my girl." Then, he again softly sang some lyrics from his hit song. "That's all right now mama, anyway you do. I need your loving. That's all right. That's all right now, mama, anyway you do."

Will it really be alright? she wondered.

Chapter Fifteen

"You agreed to cooperate!"

Being startled awake by a ringing telephone at six o'clock on a Sunday morning was enough of a shock, but hearing Sharon Eaton's shrill voice shrieking at her was as appalling as the sound of a dentist drill boring into her teeth. She sounded like a braying donkey, so Allison was obliged to hold the receiver a few inches away from her ear.

"You deliberately defied my direct order!" Sharon screamed.

"Miss Eaton . . . ."

"What's more," Sharon persisted in a piercing tone, "I don't like the way either one of you look in the newspaper picture! We spend a great deal of money cultivating our artists' images, and in one fell swoop, you've irreparably damaged our most valuable singer's persona! I'm considering taking legal action!"

"Call your artist," Allison said firmly, "and don't ever call my home number again unless I've invited you to do so."

I won't lower myself to her level by raising my voice, Allison sleepily vowed. Instead, she hung up on Sharon in the middle of her tirade, not with an angry slam of the receiver, but by simply touching the disconnect button. *Nevertheless, she'll get my point that I won't be intimidated by her or bullied into submission. As far as I'm concerned, her client has the right to do whatever he wishes, and I certainly don't have any legal obligation to cow tow to her commands!*

The rude awakening had started Allison's adrenalin coursing through her blood, and she stared wide awake at the ceiling. There was no going back to sleep, even though

Sunday was supposed to be her day of rest. She heard Karen rummaging around in the kitchen and smelled the intoxicating aroma of fresh coffee brewing.

Allison reluctantly pulled back the covers, yawned, and sat up on the side of the bed to wiggle her feet into her furry slippers. Her morning had begun with a bang, and she had to face the fact that Sharon was going to doggedly hound her every move. She contemplated the wisdom of divorcing herself from her association with her new client, who was inadvertently—through no fault of his own—tethered to the human tornado blustering through Phillip Samuels' account list. *That way, I'll be free to do whatever I want as his girlfriend. But why should I lose a valuable client because of her? Didn't Marshall and Jeff warn me that her aim was to steal my A-list clients? I shouldn't just cave in the first time she tears into me with a stabbing assault like a javelin thrower at the Olympics. I did the right thing hanging up on her. At the very least, I'm her equal in this business, not some withering subordinate who has to cower in fear every time she launches into a tirade. Who does she think she is?*

A few minutes later, she sat on a stool at their kitchen bar as Karen poured her a steaming hot cup of fresh coffee.

"I heard the phone ring," Karen said. "Do you mind me asking if everything's alright? You seem worried and lost in thought."

Allison took her first sip and then said, "Sharon Eaton called."

"At six in the morning?"

"Uh huh. She was screaming mad at me."

"What did you do, cut off her supply of hair dye?"

"Worse! I 'defied her direct order,' she said."

"Oh? And since when is she Dictator of the Universe?"

"There's a picture of me in this morning's paper that she strongly objects to. She thinks I'm sullying his reputation."

Karen picked up the morning newspaper still lying unopened on the kitchen bar. "Who would that happen to be, or do I need to ask?"

"Look on page 1 of the Entertainment section. According to her, I've now officially ruined his career."

Karen unfurled the newspaper, flipped to the entertainment section, and inspected the photo. "Oh! So I see! You're now known as 'the Mystery Mama!' Allison, let's face facts. While it's true that you only recently met, you've started seeing one of the most eligible bachelors in the city—if not the country."

"Is that a sin? Should I have all my clothes embroidered with a large 'A' like Hester Prynne in *The Scarlet Letter*?"

"There's a delicate balancing act you have to perform when you get involved with a celebrity, big or small. An entire career can literally go up in smoke overnight because of one misstep in front of the public."

"Was going out with him a misstep? Neither of us asked for our picture to be taken, much less for the newspaper to run it in a 3-column by 5-inch space!"

"I agree with you. I don't think either of you did anything wrong, and I don't see where this picture could hurt his career, but you're going to have to be more thoughtful from now on. Think of the campaign. Every piece of publicity from this day forward plays a vital part in that campaign. Maybe it's not the best thing for the public to know that 'Wonder Boy' has a steady girlfriend—especially at this critical time when we're wanting girls to fantasize about him as their own possible 'Wonder Boy.'"

"So, Sharon was right?"

"No, but you've got to be careful and take pains to see beyond the nose on your face. He's so taken with you, I'd expect you to be in seventh heaven, but don't be blinded by the clouds of joy."

"You're right. I just hope she doesn't tear into him this morning like she did with me. She might scare him off for good, and then I'd never see him again!"

"Don't bet on it. I know him, too, and I can attest to the fact that he's not the type to be easily frightened by an overbearing female."

"Are you saying that I should expect him to view Sharon Eaton the same way as we do?"

"No—probably not with our lethally explosive mixture of loathing and revulsion—but with his tongue in cheek. After all, he didn't sign a contract with Sharon. He signed a contract with Phillip Samuels. Sharon has merely infiltrated Star Records. He has a big sense of humor. I think he'll view her as if she was Milton Berle in drag and laugh her off."

Allison laughed. "I see what you mean."

Karen picked up the newspaper again. "And, by the way, did you see the article next to your photo?"

"No."

"It's all about the big soiree coming up at the Peabody Hotel, where Star Records intends to announce to the media their fall lineup of new releases."

"Oh, the formal, glittering VIP party by the pool when Sharon plans to show off her diamond-studded gown by Coco Chanel?"

Karen flipped several newspaper pages. "By the sound of this article, it seems that all of Memphis' upper crust intends to turn out that night. But there's something different about this article than some of the others you might have seen."

"What?"

"There's a picture of Miss Sharon Eaton with Anthony 'Big Bopper' Rizzo and his brother Guido."

"Let me see that," Allison demanded, grabbing the newspaper from Karen's hand. She gawked at the newspaper and gasped. "She's got her arms linked around both of them like poison ivy on a trellis! They're two of the richest men in the world!"

"And they're also reputed to be front men for the Italian Rizzo crime family."

"I can't believe this!" Allison exclaimed. "She had the nerve to call me at six o'clock in the morning to lambaste me over an innocent photo that she claims sullies the reputation of a Star Record's recording artist, when all the while she's in the same paper posing with her arms linked around racketeers! How do you like that?"

"Ah, but you were on page one, and she's on page fourteen! No wonder she was upset! Also, no one seems to know for sure if the Rizzo family is into racketeering. They're mainly considered to be two of Memphis' most eligible bachelors. They enjoy the lifestyle of the rich and famous, and the family fortune seems to be cloaked under a heavy veil of secrecy."

Allison slammed the paper down on the bar. "Why didn't you tell me about this photograph?"

Karen retorted. "I only saw it just now!"

"I wonder just how deeply involved Sharon is with the Rizzo crime family."

"I'd guess she's rather close to them," Karen thought out loud. "How else would she be in a position to be hob-knobbing with Anthony 'Big Bopper' and his brother Guido?"

Allison stared thoughtfully off into space. "There's more going on here than meets the eye, Karen. Somehow, they've helped her obtain a position on the Star Records Board of Directors."

Karen narrowed her eyes. "Who do you think actually owns that company?"

"Well, I thought it was Phillip Samuels."

"With a Board of Directors, they're bound to have other investors . . . people with big money."

"Could it be—" Allison stopped short when her mind was suddenly stunned by the thought racing through her head. "Could the Rizzo family be one of their big investors? That would explain everything! If so, those goons who were with Sharon at the Arcade and sitting like stone images while she insulted me were probably part of the same questionable group of people. They're henchmen! Now, everything's becoming clear. In her rush to glory, Sharon's taken a short cut to success, possibly becoming involved with a family that has a veiled reputation for being engaged in organized crime. To cloak her maneuvering with a shroud of respectability, she plans to attempt to ingratiate herself to high society by rubbing elbows with them in a big way!"

"I've no doubt that it's a strategic set-up to cement her social standing with all the right people."

"Several wrongs don't make a right. I'm having trouble believing that the city's upper crust will get excited about hip-swiveling rock 'n' roll singers. Liberace, maybe, but not them. It's not their style."

"She thought of that already," Karen said, still reading. "The event is being staged as a charity event."

"Of course!"

"There's more. The event's being sponsored by M&M."

"The candy manufacturer?"

"No, silly, Memphis Media. They host the annual AIM Awards, which will be that same night at the Peabody."

Allison nodded. "Advertising in Memphis. I've always wanted to be nominated. Maybe one day—"

"Your wish has come true. Here's the list of nominees, and they—oh!—get this—they include both you *and* Sharon Eaton!"

Allison's jaw dropped and she gasped. "You're kidding!"

"You've been nominated for Best Print Ad Campaign for Anderson Sportswear!"

"That's incredible!"

"And Sharon's been nominated for Rookie of the Year!"

"For what? She just arrived in town a few weeks ago!"

"Nevertheless, she's up for the award."

"I won't be surprised if she planning on attending with one of the Rizzo brothers. No wonder she bought a Chanel dress."

Karen smiled wryly. "Or, they bought one for her. Some under the table money might have also bought her that nomination, too. I'd expect at least one of the brothers to go with her if the family bought an interest in Star Records. I'm sure they'll be the center of every photographer's lens. They'll be the best-looking guys there. All the other men will be in their tuxedos, but those boys will look like they just stepped from the pages of *Esquire*."

Allison added, "And all the women will be prancing around in elegant, floor length gowns and showing off their most expensive jewelry. It sounds like a dangerous kind of gathering to hold beside a swimming pool, if you ask me. Like you said, someone just might fall in!"

Both women giggled.

Chapter Sixteen

"There's only one thing to do," Allison told Karen. "I've got to show up at the AIM awards with the #1 new artist in the nation, and we'll have to somehow sweep the media's interest so that Sharon's coup d'état sinks like the *Titanic*!"

"Why not go one better and get him on national TV the same night . . . ."

In unison, both sisters gasped and then shouted, "On *The Ed Sullivan Show*!"

"We're thinking alike, sister. Imagine the impact of him being on the show at 7:00 the same night he makes an in-person appearance at the AIM Awards with you!"

Allison grabbed her telephone. "Daddy thinks he only moved to New York to manage the show's national advertising staff. I bet he never imagined that he'd be in a position to help out his daughters in a big way!"

Later that morning, Karen left to have brunch with a friend. Allison decided to begin her bath, but she kept being delayed. Seven times, the telephone rang with one friend after another calling to congratulate her on her nomination for the AIM Award. When Karen returned briefly, Allison was still fielding calls.

"I'm not sticking around for this," Karen declared. "It's going to be a circus around here all day. I'll see you this evening."

Finally the calls subsided. With a little time to herself, Allison was able to take a relaxing bath. She had just finished, stepped from the tub, and wrapped herself in a bath sheet when the doorbell rang. When she opened the door to the hall she discovered a large, professionally wrapped package from a local florist. She picked the package up and brought it into the kitchen where she tore the wrapping and discovered inside a lovely flower

arrangement, a vase containing 100 blooms of Autumn Peruvian Lilies. She pulled out the little attached card, opened the envelope, and read:
"These are only half as beautiful as you.
Thank you for the best day of my life,
and congrats on your nomination.
I'll see you soon."

Instead of a signature, he had drawn a little guitar. Of course, she knew who had sent them. She put the arrangement on her dresser across from her bed, where she was able to admire and appreciate his selection. The flowers were truly lovely and their wonderful fragrance added a cheery note to a room grossly in need of merriment. She was finding escaping from the cloud that Sharon had cast over her life difficult, but the flowers—and the nomination—helped buoy her spirit.

Another interruption came with another knock on the door.

More flowers! she presumed. Before turning the knob, she asked, "Who's there?"

"It's me."

It's him! She clutched the towel that was about to fall loose, and her heart leapt. The sound of his voice always caused her to go weak in the knees. There was no one she wished to be with more, but once again, he had caught her off guard and she was not ready to receive company. *Still, I can't reject him and leave him standing out in the hall!* She could not contain her excitement, and she laughed, partly out of nervousness and partly out of sheer delight. She called out, "What are you doing here?"

"I said in the note I'd see you soon, didn't I?"

"This is sooner than I expected."

"Aren't you going to invite me in?"

She quickly brushed her hair back in an attempt to look poised and presentable and said, "Just a minute!"

She ran to her bedroom, grabbed her robe, and quickly slung it around herself, tying the belt as she raced back. She took a deep breath and opened the door.

"As always, you look terrific!" he declared, giving her a big, friendly hug.

"If you'd call me next time before coming over, I'll be much more presentable. Still, I'm glad to see you!"

Wasting no time making himself immediately at home, he sat down on the couch. Allison followed. Despite the fact that he had decided to arrive with no advance warning, she felt the least she could do was be cordial, especially considering how attentive he was being. She forgot about the robe she wore and her bare feet, until she went back to the bedroom to get the floral arrangement to use as a center piece. She brought the arrangement into the living room and placed them where they would look their best, which seemed like the right thing to do.

"I just had to see you this morning," he said. "We were so busy last night we didn't read the whole newspaper. After I got wind of the announcement about your nomination, I just had to tell you how proud I am of you. I told you before that you're the best, and now this proves it!"

Allison laughed. He was irresistible to her. His mannerisms. His attentiveness. His way of cutting to the chase. The loose curl hanging over his tanned forehead. Once again, she found herself as comfortable with him as he was with her.

"Do you want to see some of the things I've been working on?."

"No," he replied immediately. "That can wait. I've put in my time today. I'm ready for some relaxation and recreation. I haven't had a good back rub in a while. Will you give me one?"

Before she could answer, he turned his back to her. She was somewhat surprised that he would suddenly request such a personal thing, but since friends help friends, she started to massage his shoulders.

"Mmm. This feels so nice. But would you mind if I took off my shirt? It would feel even nicer if your fingers and hands were rubbing directly on my skin."

He unbuttoned his shirt, figuring she would go along with his request. In one swoop, his knit shirt was over his head and discarded.

With his shirt off, Allison admired more closely his strong, well-developed build. She knew before that he took good care of himself, but she could not have imagined the perfect development of his muscles that were only observable without clothes. She began to massage his neck and shoulders again. *I wonder what kind of sports or exercise he participates in to maintain his hard, muscular body. It's so titillating and enjoyable to see and touch his masculine frame. I'm glad that he can't see my face. He'd know what I was thinking!*

Allison rubbed and massaged his back carefully paying attention to every inch of skin and muscle. She gave of herself as she wished he would have had the situation been reversed, and while she thought he could not possibly know what she was thinking and feeling as she worked, he did. He knew by the gentle and loving way she touched him.

"That's enough," he finally told her, still wanting more but also wanting to be considerate of her. "You must be getting tired."

Allison wanted to tell him that she would be happy to continue, that the moments she was spending with him were the most joyous she had experienced in a long time. She wanted to say that, but she knew she would never be able to summon up the courage. She also recognized by the tone in his voice that it was best to do as he directed her. While her fingers might normally have begun to ache after such a strenuous exercise, she noticed no strain, and was only disappointed that he was stopping her. She liked touching him more than she would have wanted to admit.

He turned around to face her and teased, "How much of a good thing can a man take? I'm glad you're so good at back rubs!"

Allison's eyes met his, and as always seemed to happen when she was with him, she began to blush. She averted her gaze as quickly as possible once she realized how she was responding. She was embarrassed to find herself staring at his well-developed chest, muscular pecs, and rounded shoulders, and she wondered what he must be thinking of her.

"Now it's my turn to give you a rub down!"

"I didn't realize that this was a reciprocal situation," Allison answered, surprised at his offer.

"You scratch my back, I'll scratch yours."

Allison smiled brightly in response and lay down on the floor, while he drew himself up close to her. With his left thigh resting against her right side, he loosened her robe and slid his strong hands inside.

Only then did she realize the provocative situation she had put herself in. She was glad that, as of yet, he was not trying to take advantage of her. She did not know what she would do if he tried. She felt his strong and powerful hands gently do their work. He was as attentive to her as she had been to him. His fingers prodded, nudged, lightly grazed, and rubbed, delivering sensual pleasures she had never realized could be derived from a back massage. When he reached the lower limits of her back, she half wished he would move on to her buttocks, but he did not. At first, she assumed that he was being a gentleman. Then, she wondered if he merely wanted to tease her. When his fingers lightly danced across the sides of her breasts, she knew that he wanted to do more than tease. His touch was ecstasy. He wanted her just as she wanted him.

He gently rolled her over on her back. With sensitivity to her and respect of her modest nature, he carefully managed to leave her loosely fastened robe closed. He swiftly pulled himself on top of her, being careful to support himself so she would not feel crushed beneath the weight of his body.

"I think I'm falling in love with you, Allison." He whispered the words as tenderly as he knew how.

"Don't." Allison tried to stop him from saying more. She was not sure why, but somehow she knew she was not ready to deal with this from him, even though she knew that he was feeling exactly what she was feeling.

"Why should I stop? I've waited for—even tried to bring about a time that would be right to tell you what I really feel, and this seems like the right time. I'm not going to stop now. I want you more than any woman I've ever known. When I'm not with you, you're all I find myself thinking about."

He lowered his head and kissed her with a longing she had never known before. He was loving and passionate all at once. His lips began to search her body, nibbling at her neck and ear lobes. He continued to embrace her tenderly and Allison surprised herself with the openness with which she enjoyed every moment they were sharing. She realized that the intensity of their physical encounter was about to become more serious.

Chapter Seventeen

"Allison! Allison!"

Karen's voice was all too easy to ignore. She had heard her timber and tone all her life, and she was quite adept at tuning her out when she wished. At the moment, she chose to pay no attention. Thinking of the day before had lulled her into a glorious stupor. She remembered feeling him loosen her robe, his strong and powerful hands gently massaging her body, and the words of love the two of them exchanged, so soft and tender, sending her somewhere she had never been before. She had to smile when recalling how she first assumed that he was just being a gentleman and merely teasing her when his fingers lightly danced across the sides of her breasts, but that was the beginning of what turned out to be more than a tease. He was all man, and his touch was ecstasy. He had wanted to fulfill her, and she had wanted him to. She sighed. The memory of every moment she spent with him would remain with her for a lifetime.

"Allison!" Karen persisted. "How can I direct you if you're not listening?"

Allison shook her head as if waking from a deep sleep. "What did you say? Am I doing something wrong?"

"I know you're not a professional model, but you'll do just fine if you'll listen to me. Move when I tell you to move, okay?"

Allison responded apologetically. "Sure. I guess my mind just started to wander."

The photography session had been going extraordinarily well. Luckily, the weather was holding up, which meant that their work would be completed fast like they wanted. Their father had vowed to do everything he could to secure a few minutes on *The Ed Sullivan Show* for the band.

Fortunately, he had a good reason to request the booking: they had a hit song that was moving up the charts and gaining national exposure in record time. From state to state, disc jockeys were jumping on board with the rock 'n' roll craze, an unusual occurrence for stations that had previously only played music that sounded like leftovers from their parent's generation. Yet, the new sound was not to be ignored, and securing a spot on *The Ed Sullivan Show* was sure to bring the revolutionary new sound to the masses, as well as be the greatest blessing of their lives.

Karen shot picture after picture of Allison at minutely different angles. "We have to get the big promotional picture to Dad tonight, which means I've got to spend hours with the developer creating a composite that blends some adoring girls looking at the band's lead singer. We've got the first two done, so now if we can just get this third one at the right angle, we'll be done!"

Karen's idea was terrific. In fact, the entire reformulation of the campaign had taken a dramatic turn and was sure to draw the right kind of attention. This new angle brought them an opportunity of a lifetime, and Allison wanted to make sure she did her part right.

She posed carefully, even though her neck was beginning to hurt. She finally asked, "Have you got enough?"

Karen snapped one more and lowered her camera. "I think we can call it a day. Somewhere in all these, we'll have exactly the right angle that fits the picture yet obscures your face."

"Fine," Allison agreed, finally relaxing. She was exhausted, never having imagined how strenuous modeling really was. This was probably the only time she would ever be asked to model for a national ad, and were the cause not for the man she loved, she would not have done so. She was a copywriter and a designer. True, she was also pretty, and with her hair pulled back in a pony tail and her back to the camera, she could easily pass for one of the teenage girls who were going gaga over the singer they were hearing on the radio.

Within the hour, they were back inside their rented studio, where Karen disappeared into the dark room to develop film. Allison posted herself at a light table and was pouring over the prints and negatives from their recent session when, unbeknownst to her, two dark-suited men appeared at the door behind her and let themselves in. They were both young and tall, and they seemed grimly studious. They observed her in silence for about a minute, and then one of them wordlessly nudged the other and nodded in her direction. They quietly approached her.

"Are you Allison Webster?"

Startled, she looked around at them.

"We're looking for Allison Webster," he repeated.

She was taken aback by their stealthy intrusion, but instantly realized that the men were not the type to be hanging around a building that was usually populated with flamboyant artists and overly chatty advertising clients. She moved her chair aside and stood. "I'm Allison."

"I'm Special Agent-in-Charge Wilkins, and this is Special Agent Walker. We'd like to ask you a few questions."

"Who are you with?"

"The Federal Bureau of Investigation." They pulled out their identification to reassure her.

Allison was momentarily stunned, but her good manners rose to the fore. She gestured toward the sofa and said "Please sit down."

Wilkins and Walker filed over to the sofa and sat, but both men leaned forward expectantly, as if they were not planning to relax. Walker pulled out a note pad and pen.

Allison sat at a chair sideways to the sofa. She wanted to speak, but was uncomfortable to the point of not knowing whether to voice a pleasantry or merely wait for them to speak first. She opted to wait.

Wilkins spoke unsmilingly and maintained steady eye contact with her. "A series of offenses has been brought to our attention and classified. Our goal is to expose, disrupt, misdirect, discredit, or otherwise neutralize the activities of certain individuals and organizations whose ideas or goals the government opposes. Our investigation has definitely established the identity of certain offenders, and there's a reasonable indication that an organization or person meets the guidelines for an investigation. May we ask you a few questions?"

"Yes."

"According to our contacts in the recording industry, you have an affiliation with individuals in that industry. Is that true?"

"Yes."

"To what extent have you developed such relationships? I assume you know between three and five people working in that area?"

"I think I know only two locally."

"We have information that indicates some local Memphis recording studios are pursuing a number of different genre artists. Would you agree?"

"The industry seems to be moving in some new directions, if that's what you mean."

"Off the record, Miss Webster, are you involved with Phillip Samuels?"

"Not really. Not yet. I would sure like to be, but I'm not yet his Agent of Record."

"How would you obtain that opportunity? Everybody knows that his company has never gotten deeply involved with exploitation on a national scale and can't fulfill large orders."

Allison cleared her throat and then said, "I wouldn't say I will get any opportunity, sir, although I might take the liberty to contact him."

"Why would you want to work with his clients? Isn't it true that most Memphis artists have questionable talent?"

"Well, I wouldn't say that. I think some of them are very talented!"

Wilkins barely smiled. "We're new to this field and could use all the help we can get. How does this business work with yours?"

"I help with a lot of local business, creating marketing campaigns that assist them in achieving their sales goals. I visualize mainly print ads, and I create PR campaigns to get the public to respond the way companies want. That's what marketing is all about."

"You're considered to be good at what you do?"

Allison laughed. "Some people think so."

"Who would that be?"

"My clients do. I think the industry does, too. I've just been nominated for an industry award."

"Some people are more prominent in the industry than others?"

"Yes, that's true in every line of work."

"Do you know anyone named Eaton?"

"There's a Sharon Eaton."

"And she's who?"

"She's a Nashville advertising executive who recently transplanted here to Memphis."

"You're good friends?"

"Hardly!"

"Do you work for her?"

Allison paused, and then carefully said, "I am working *with her* on one account, in the loosest sense of the word. We have a mutual client, who she seems to think she has a right to manipulate. I'm certainly not working *for her* at all."

At that moment, a telephone rang in the developing rooms. They heard Karen call, "I'll get it!"

"And has she ever revealed to you the extent of her involvement with local record manufacturing?"

Allison shook her head. "No."

"What will happen if you're no longer involved with her?"

Allison was unsure how to answer. "I don't expect much would happen. As I said, I'm not really involved with her on any project, other than the one that, in my opinion, she shouldn't be involved with at all. That's a matter that's still up in the air."

"There's no way you could avoid working with her if she would be more in control of these kind of projects?"

"Well," Allison laughed nervously, "I don't think I'd care to pursue any project where I had to have a direct one on one involvement with her. I can always turn down a job. I'm an independent consultant."

"Would she be expected to be involved with a variety of industry clients?"

"I guess so."

"Did you see the photo of her in today's paper? Will you comment on her involvement with the Rizzo family?"

"I can't. I don't know anything definite about that. You probably know more than I do."

"Would you tell us about her affiliation with the AIM group and any other of her friends, family, vendors, subsidiaries, or competitors?"

"Sir, I don't know anything more about her."

Karen, who was still busy in the back and did not know that Allison was talking to the FBI men, called out, "Allison! That was Sharon Eaton who called! You're invited to a big meeting at Star Records tomorrow morning at eight o'clock. I told her that I wasn't your social secretary and that she'd have to talk directly to you. She seemed snippy. You better call her when you get a chance!"

Wilkins and Walker could not help but overhear Karen, and they exchanged knowing glances.

Wilkins said, "I think you would be smart to make that call when you get a chance. We'd like to ask you to go to that meeting. We'd appreciate your help if you'd let us know any information you learn. Can we count on you?"

Allison took a deep breath, instantly feeling somewhat frightened and suspecting that she was being drawn into an ugly whirlpool of intrigue. Even so, she and Karen had already deduced that Sharon was perhaps sticking her finger too deeply into pies that a more prudent person would avoid, and since she did not consider Sharon to be her friend, she decided that the best course of action was to cooperate., "Do you have a card?" Allison asked.

Chapter Eighteen

"Rizzo, Luigi?"

"Present."

"Vittorino, Alfredo?"

"Present."

"Webster, Allison?"

"Present." Allison softly cleared her throat after answering the Secretary, who was calling the role at the Star Records Board of Directors Meeting. She laid her pen down on top of a closed manila folder she had brought that contained her campaign layouts and a set of the recent photographs Karen had taken, and she could barely swallow what she had just heard. *"Rizzo? Vittorino? Who are those Italian men? Is it just a coincidence for that man to have the same last name of the infamous family reputed to be involved with racketeering?"* She had anticipated the meeting to be overloaded with information, but that surprise left her momentarily stunned. She thought, *There sure are a large number of people here. The room's overfilled, and I get the feeling that they're all here because of something important. There must be far-reaching implications, or why else would they have asked me to come?* As she gazed at their faces, she only recognized a few, and she, the secretary, and Sharon Eaton were the only women in the entire group of thirty.

The secretary continued reading from her alphabetical attendee list. "Williamson, Maximillian?"

"Present."

"Yaranski, James?"

"Present."

"Yates, Gale?"

"Present."

"Mr. President, all members and guests are present and accounted for."

Phillip Samuels nodded his head and forced a smile over his grim face. He coughed once, adjusted his tie, and shifted his position in his chair. The man did not look happy.

Allison sat next to a small, wiry, nervous sort of man with a bald spot covering half his head and rimless glasses perched over his overly large nose. She noticed that he sat with his hands protectively on top of a manila file folder with the words "Investment Summary" on the tab.

The Secretary stood and announced, "The Board recognizes Harold Stein, Chairman of the Board."

As a dour-faced, heavy-set man rose and went to the head of the conference table, Allison glanced at Sharon, who straightened her spine, tilted her head high, and leaned forward. She had dressed in a stunning business suit with a smart black jacket and matching Ponte skirt that fit her impeccably. The long buttoned sleeves and welt pockets offered added details that made the suit look unique, while the one-button jacket left the lapels gaping open, revealing her ample bust barely contained beneath a low-cut cream-colored lacey knit blouse. The effect was serious yet sensual. *Obviously, Sharon's dressed to wow the other Board Members*, Allison observed, *or is she trying to gloss over her crude and overbearing personality? And why is she grinning and radiating such glamour and confidence?*

"I'm pleased to begin our meeting with an announcement of great importance to this Board," Mr. Stein began. "May I introduce our new appointee to the position of Vice President of Sales and Marketing . . . Miss Sharon Eaton!"

Sharon shot a demure smile at those around the table, as their generous applause burst forth. She stood, approached the head of the table, and shook hands with Mr. Stein.

"Thank you, Mr. Chairman, Members of the Board, Madame Secretary, and guests. I'm honored to be a new, vital force in Star Record's success. This year, we launch an unprecedented roster of new talent, with a goal in mind to carry our tradition of excellence and cutting-edge artistry to new levels. Being #1 in an evolving industry looms as more than a mere goal; it heralds a new era, one in which we can chart the course for future developments, as well as lead the industry as the trend setter of record."

Sharon consciously moved her eyes around the table as she continued. "With those objectives at heart, no one will be surprised to find that growth—and the growing pains that accompany that expansion—will prove challenging, but I stand firm in the belief that I share with Mr. Stein, the Board, and our investors, that branching out into new fields invites us to rise to the apex of our abilities. As Vice President of Sales and Marketing, I vow to trim expenses, tighten our control of campaigns, and effectively initiate a new standard, one that will guide our sales team to set new records in retailing."

Now, Sharon pointedly fixed her gaze squarely on Allison. "Bringing our advertising and marketing in house will give us the advantage of maintaining a singular, guiding approach to campaign designs. I will bring to each artist the same commitment to excellence that has been the hallmark of my career, the standard to which others will wish to achieve, and the trademark that has just earned me the honor of being nominated for the AIM Rookie of the Year Award, even though I'm no rookie in this business. You all know the value of my fifteen-year track record of success, one that I now offer as a feature of my association with Star Records. Thank you for the opportunity to become a critical component of our future accomplishments. Victory is not merely at hand; our triumph has already begun!"

Everyone present suddenly burst into applause, unanimous in their outpouring of approval. One by one, they began to stand while they clapped, and when the wiry man sitting next to her shot to his feet, Allison stood, too. Unfortunately, in his rush to jump up, the man's arm brushed haphazardly against the corner of his manila folder and swept the folder over the edge of the table. Papers flew out at Allison's feet. She immediately stooped to pick up the folder, while the man awkwardly tried to assist. When she reached for several pages that had scattered beyond his reach, she could not help but see some of the information. One document particularly caught her eye: Investment Summary of Rizzo Corp. As she lifted the page, her eyes scanned down the document and she saw the figure "$1,275,000 51% share" inked into a blank beside the words "Capital Investment."

"Here you are," she quickly said to the man, before she had actually gathered up the loose papers. She turned her back to him as she was picked up the last few documents. That gave her three fleeting seconds more to glance at the Rizzo document and confirm that she was not imagining what she saw before she swept the paper into a stack with the others. Then she stood and said, "It's a little crowded in here today, isn't it?" She smiled and handed the folder and papers back to him.

Over the applause, the Secretary loudly announced to the group, "That concludes the public portion of today's meeting. Board Members, please adjourn to the private conference room on the second floor for our Annual Review."

Allison was practically overwhelmed by the impact of the startling revelations she had just witnessed. *Not only am I going to be shoved out of any future advertising contracts, what with Sharon taking advertising and marketing "in house," a euphemism I interpret to really mean "into her clutches," but that Italian family has clearly infiltrated Star*

Records and made a major investment in the company, no doubt to secure their stranglehold on all operations!

The Secretary strained to make eye contact with Allison and waved at her. "Miss Webster! May I see you for a moment before you leave?"

The room began to clear and a path opened for Allison to approach her. "You wanted to see me?"

"I have your invitation here," she replied, reaching into her satchel.

"My invitation?"

She extended an envelope to Allison. "To the AIM Awards."

Allison was puzzled, but took the envelope. "Why would you have my invitation?"

"Miss Eaton handed it to me today before the meeting."

"Was it sent to her by mistake?"

"Oh no. She brought it from B&B."

"But why—"

"Maybe you haven't heard," the Secretary smiled. "Miss Eaton's company just merged with B&B."

"Oh?"

"I'll see you at the awards. By the way, congratulations on your nomination!"

"Thank you."

If a truck had collided with her, Allison could not have felt more stricken. She left the conference room and made a beeline to the elevator with the aim of distancing herself from the place as quickly as possible. Too much in shock to even voice pleasantries to anyone she passed, she needed space and time to digest the full impact of the scandalous disclosures she had just absorbed.

Tears welled up in her eyes, as she fished around in her purse and withdrew Agent Wilkins' business card.

Chapter Nineteen

"Guido Rizzo is romancing Binnie Barnes," Karen announced.

Allison had just opened their apartment door. The television was blaring again, and Karen was lounging on the couch. Allison looked at her, stunned again for the sixth time in one morning. Her mind still reeled from having witnessed Sharon Eaton publicly acknowledging her promotion to the office of Vice President of Sales and Marketing at Star Records. She was still in shock over hearing that their advertising decisions would now be dictated exclusively by Sharon through some kind of cozy in-house agency arrangement. She had not yet gotten over being astonished about the Secretary telling her that Sharon had also maneuvered to merge her start-up Memphis agency with the town's venerable marketing institution, B&B. She remained astounded over seeing the Investment Summary of Rizzo Corp. document with its $1,275,000 investment figure that apparently bought them a 51% controlling interest in Star Records. Now, this news about Guido Rizzo romancing the owner of B&B came as the final blow in a morning that had been characterized by her dodging one land mine after another.

"Where have you been?" Karen asked. "You look like a lost puppy on a street corner!"

"I've been to the Star Records Board of Directors Meeting. I could use some *good* news for a change."

"Well, my news is good, that is if you're Binnie Barnes. She's in Seventh Heaven, but you look like you've been through Hell."

Allison set down her purse and pulled off her scarf. "Is it that obvious?"

"Don't tell me—let me guess—they announced that Mahalia Jackson and Ella Fitzgerald are recording a duet of "Rock Around the Clock?"

"Worse. Sharon Eaton has virtually taken over Star Records. She's the new VP of Sales. She's cutting off all contracts with outside agencies, which will leave me high and dry. She's merged her own agency with B&B. And I would have made Nancy Drew proud today, when I surreptitiously spied documents that verified that the Rizzo family recently bought a controlling interest in Star Records!"

Karen flipped off the television. "That explains a lot of things! What are you going to do next—work for the FBI as an industrial spy?"

Allison ignored Karen's quip. "Sharon's unfathomable nomination for Rookie of the Year now seems understandable. From what you just informed me, Guido Rizzo is romancing Binnie Barnes. Binnie, who owns B&B—the official sponsor of the AIM Awards—just happens to be on the award nominating committee. B&B is now at least partly owned by Sharon, who probably used her clout to leverage Binnie and the others on the nominating committee to nominate her, and she also now works full-time for Star Records. Star Records' controlling investor just happens to be Rizzo Corp. They all make for a cozy set of bedfellows! Marshall told me she'd stop at nothing to get what she wanted, and he was right! And both Sharon and the Rizzo family are being investigated by the FBI for racketeering crimes!"

"Yes, Sharon seems to be a busy bee," Karen agreed, "but does she have a date tonight with a handsome young singer who's making his network TV debut on *The Ed Sullivan Show*?"

Allison's jaw dropped and she finally had to sit down. She looked at Karen in disbelief.

Karen said, "See? You needed some good news and now you have good news. In fact, you have *great* news! Dad called. He confirmed the booking! A three-minute time slot. The segment will be broadcast live from WHMM-TV here in Memphis on Sunday at 7:00 p.m., the same Sunday night as the AIM Awards! What's more, our photo mural is ready and looks great!"

Karen ran to her bedroom, but she immediately returned gently dragging a life-size cardboard cutout blow-up of the entire band. The image showed the sensational quartette in full performance with what appeared to be three teenage girls in the foreground gleefully enjoying them. The girls were actually Allison in the three shots Karen had taken and painstakingly merged into a composite with the other photo of the band.

Karen asked proudly, "What do you think?"

For the second time in twenty-four hours, tears began to well up in Allison's eyes.

"Are you kidding? It's marvelous! I'm so excited! Can you imagine how he's going to respond to this? You're a genius!"

"Oh, it's just a matter of knowing when to snap the button."

"You're being uncharacteristically modest."

"I'm just a photographer who's had a lot of experience and likes what she does. Besides, you were there to push me into giving just a little bit more than usual. And, you won't have to wait long to see how he responded. He came by. He brought you this." Karen handed Allison a note in an envelope.

"What's that?"

"Open it."

Allison opened the note. She read, "Come with me to dinner tonight. I'll pick you up at eight. Let's celebrate tonight by dining at Suzette's!" The note was signed with a hand-drawn guitar. Now, for the third time in twenty-four hours, her eyes began to fill with tears.

She glowed when she revealed to Karen, "He wants to take me to Suzette's tonight at eight! I've never been there. It's one of Memphis' most romantic restaurants!"

Karen said, "I know Suzette's. It's the kind of place a guy will take you when he's going to propose. He already saw the mural, but I didn't tell him about Daddy's surprise. I saved that one for you. You should both have a lot to talk about tonight!"

Allison looked lovingly at the life-size image of him on the mural and said, "I could just kiss him!"

"Something tells me you already have."

"I'd be lying to you if I said we hadn't kissed," Allison admitted. "Well, we did more than kiss."

"It's nice with someone you love, isn't it?"

Allison wanted to make sure that Karen did not get the wrong impression. "We didn't sleep together, Karen. I find him more attractive and exciting than any man I've ever known. He's handsome. He's intelligent. He's attentive. And soon he'll be successful. Why did this have to happen to me?"

"If word gets out that he's going to be at WHMM-TV, there'll be seven hundred other girls asking 'Why *isn't* this happening to me?' I don't get it. You should be overjoyed. What you're describing to me—isn't that what every woman's looking for? A meaningful relationship with an attractive man who adores her?"

Allison wiped the tears from her eyes. "You're right. I should start getting ready. What time is it?"

"One o'clock. You've got seven hours to get ready. Now, about those other seven hundred girls . . . don't you think we'd all be better off if the station wasn't stampeded the night he and the band do their segment?"

"Absolutely. We'll have to tell the station not to announce it." Allison insisted.

"They'll want to announce it, alright. That's the kind of news you couldn't keep quiet if Campbell's Soup canned it. They can sell a lot of ads around the live broadcast. But, they can discretely require their advertisers to sign a confidentiality agreement to mums the word and the station can withhold an announcement until a half hour before air time. Something tells me that alone will bring out a crowd—smaller maybe—say only a few hundred. Besides, don't you want him to accompany you to the AIM Awards right after that?"

"He wouldn't miss it."

"The TV station will be covering that, too, I'm sure. In fact, between the two events, you'll be surrounded by more cameras than Marilyn Monroe!"

"I'll have to get something to wear! I've been so busy that I hadn't taken the time to think about it."

"We'll go shopping this weekend and find the perfect gown!"

Allison retreated to her bedroom. She had been working extremely hard, and she was overdue for some fun. She was ecstatic that he thought enough to take her out on a week night, and she could not have wished for any occasion more appropriate to celebrate *The Ed Sullivan Show* booking for him and the band to perform for three minutes. *Three minutes! Just fleeting moments to some, but a life-changing event to us! Who knows what will happen in the wake of such a tremendous moment in a performer's profession? Careers have been made or broken by less time than that on national television. This is a lifetime opportunity!*

She had not counted on keeping her mouth shut about such a tremendous blessing, but Karen was right. They had a responsibility to let him enjoy his moment of glory without any troublesome roadblocks, no matter how much fun could be had by telling everyone she knew in advance.

She reread his note again, as if she was in a dream. *It's like receiving a note from Prince Charming, and he signed the note with his special signature, a little guitar that means love!* She knew that he cared for her more than anyone else in the world, and she longed to be with him more than she dared to admit. She felt short of breath and her body tingled all over. She wanted to scream out with shrieks of joy and elation. She wanted to cry again because she was so unsure about what was going to happen next. *So what if Sharon Eaton shoves me out of the promotional side of his career like someone would discard a plate of objectionable food? I have a bond with him that no one can sever, and I'm sure that will be true forever.* She carefully folded the note and pressed it gently against her heart.

With glee, Allison fairly danced around the bedroom and bath, as she prepared for another glorious date with the most desirable man in Memphis. While she bathed, rolled her hair, and generally pampered and polished herself, her thoughts turned to daydreams. She wondered just when he would appear at her door. *Probably at the moment the clock strikes eight, punctual to perfection, as usual.* She imagined what he might be wearing. *Nothing shocking like his blue suede shoes, but probably something casual/dressy with a jacket and a silk open-neck shirt with big lapels, something that'll be appropriate for the intimate, well-appointed dining room at Suzette's, Memphis' oldest and most idyllic restaurant with candlelit tables by high windows that have breathtaking views of the Mississippi River. I'm the luckiest girl in the world!*

At precisely eight o'clock, their doorbell rang. Karen answered, and there he stood—framed by the doorway and wearing beige pleated trousers and a matching beige open-neck silk shirt with wide lapels that spread over a smart blue silk tweed jacket. He might have been a fashion plate for *Esquire*. He smiled widely when he saw Karen and bent over slightly to kiss her. For a fleeting moment, she wished she was still dating him, but she managed to keep her passion dormant and call Allison.

A few minutes later when they drove away, they were quickly lost in talk and looking only at each other. Neither of them noticed a dark sedan parked on the street beneath deep shadows cast by a large spreading oak tree. The vehicle quietly pulled away from the curb and stealthily followed them from a discrete distance.

Chapter Twenty

"We have a reservation for two."

The Maitre d' at Suzette's nodded and asked, "May I have your name please?"

"Ilikeike."

He scanned down his reservation list. "Ah! Here it is. Please follow me Mr. Ilikeike."

Allison tried her best to control a determined giggle, as they were ushered through the dim lighting and soft piano music of Suzette's dining room. She floated through the room wearing an iridescent mint taffeta and tulle dress that featured a cuffed, strapless bodice lined in marquisette and boned, with a pleated tulle bust overlay and pointed waist. When she passed people who turned their heads for a second look, they saw a matching bow with sash streaming down her back from the rear neckline and cascading softly across a multi-layered tulle skirt with a pellon-backed taffeta panel. The dress contrasted beautifully with her long wavy red hair.

As soon as they were seated at a gorgeous table for two in front of a high window overlooking a spectacular panorama of the Mississippi River and Downtown Memphis, she leaned forward and jokingly asked, "Mr. Ilikeike?"

"I've had to stop using my real name," he explained. "Girls find out and seem to sort of drop from the ceiling and surround me. I got 'Ilikeike' from an Eisenhower campaign button. So far, no one's got wind of it!"

Allison chuckled and cast her eyes around the intimate, well-appointed dining room that featured fine woodwork and high ceilings, as well as original artwork and abundant fresh flowers that adorned every table. She softly said, "You picked a lovely spot!"

"Do you like the flowers?" he asked, pointing to the soothing mix of red roses, chrysanthemums, and greenery in a green glass cube in front of them.

"I love them!"

"I asked Karen to call me while you were taking your bath and tell me the color of the dress you planned to wear. I called the restaurant and asked them to put the roses in a matching vase on the table."

"You're so sweet!"

He gazed at her admiringly "You look like a picture on the cover of a magazine!"

As if on cue, the restaurant's photographer appeared from out of nowhere. "May I take the lady's and gentleman's picture?"

Of course, Allison was instantly flattered and they both readily posed. The photographer took only two shots so as not to create too much of a disturbance in front of the other diners.

The photographer said, "If you'll give your address to the Maitre d' on your way out later, we'll send you a set of color prints!"

"Thank you!" they both replied at the same time.

Allison was nearly overjoyed. "That was so thoughtful of you to arrange the exquisite flowers in a vase to match my dress! Tonight seems to be an evening full of surprises!"

"There'll be more," he said with a wide grin, looking down shyly at one of the candles and chuckling for a fleeting moment. As often happened, a lock of hair tumbled loose and dangled over his forehead in a most becoming fashion that Allison could not help but notice and admire. He reached a tanned hand into his side coat pocket and fished out a small box. Allison instantly recognized the box as a jewelry case, and she was immediately breathless. Time seemed to stand still, as her mind raced to anticipate what he was about to say or do.

"There's something I wanted to ask you before the waiter comes over."

"Yes?"

"What things make you really happy, Allison?"

She needed no time to think up an answer. "Just being with you makes me really happy. When we're together, like tonight."

He opened the jewelry box and revealed a double heart diamond promise ring. "I hope if I give you this promise ring you'll be even happier. Look at this every time you might doubt me, and you'll remember that I promised to always be faithful to you."

For the fourth time that day, Allison's eyes misted with tears, her heart beat picked up, and she found that even the simple act of breathing took all the self-control she could summon. Had she not been seated, she would have sworn that the room had begun to swirl.

He gently took her hand and slipped the ring on her finger. The band fit perfectly. Then, he lifted her hand to his lips and kissed the ring. His lips also brushed her skin, and she felt a tingling sensation that radiated in waves through her entire arm.

"Thank you!" she blushed. "That's the nicest moment I've ever known. I'll cherish this every day for the rest of my life."

At that second, someone at a table across the restaurant shouted "Look!" and pointed toward the windows. All eyes turned at once to look out at the nighttime sky, where they saw an enormous shooting star streak through the heavens in a brilliant flash. In another second, the meteor vanished.

He whispered, "They say that for every falling star, another star is born."

Allison remembered the big announcement she had wished to surprise him with, and this moment seem preordained to reveal her secret to him. "I told you that tonight seemed to be an evening full of surprises. You know my father. He lives in New York now and works for *The Ed Sullivan Show*. This Sunday at nine o'clock is the AIM Awards at the Peabody Hotel here in Memphis, but across America two hours earlier, the whole nation will be watching *you and your band make your network television debut!* Daddy's got you booked for a three-minute performance of your new hit that'll be broadcast coast-to-coast live from WFMM-TV right here! Sunday night, a new star will be born, just like you said!"

He took a deep breath, threw his head back, and smiled so wide that his teeth looked like a piano keyboard. He barely was able to say "Excuse me just a minute . . . ."

Inexplicably, he rose and rushed through a nearby swinging door to the kitchen. Suddenly, she heard the muffled sound of him screaming "Woopee!" One of the chefs was so startled by his unexpected intrusion and outburst that he dropped a steaming pan of lobsters.

The door swung open again, and he returned to their table by the window, appearing as calm as if he had just returned from making a telephone call, but now there were two telltale curls dangling over his forehead. Half the diners were looking perplexed at each other and wondering where the shout had come from, and no one suspected that he had nearly blown the chef down in his excitement and joy.

A waiter approached them and asked, "Is everything alright, sir?"

"Everything's peachy!"

Allison agreed. "This is the happiest night of our lives!"

The waiter dryly asked, "Would you like to order now, or would you like to next try shouting loud enough to bring down our dining room chandelier?"

They all three laughed, but then he said apologetically, "I'm sorry about the mess in the kitchen. Put those crabs on my bill, will you?"

"They're not crabs, sir. They're lobsters."

"They could be a bunch of crawdads, for all I care. Tell the staff to enjoy them on me! We're celebrating tonight!"

"Yes sir. I'll bring your menus shortly."

After the waiter had gone, Allison was stunned when he impulsively leaned across the flowers and candles and kissed her. She was startled by his impetuousness, but that did not stop him from saying, "I wish this night could go on forever."

"Me, too."

"I don't want to ever let you go." He took both of her hands in his. "I can't believe this is happening. It seems like forever that I've been waiting for this to happen . . . to meet a girl like you, and to finally get a break after all these years of trying so hard to get somewhere."

He gazed into her eyes with an intense longing that was strange and wonderful. Allison could not believe how much she was enjoying being with him, and wearing his promise ring felt like the fulfillment of a fantasy. She had not intended for this to happen, but for the moment, she was happier than she had ever been, glad to be holding hands with the man she wanted to spend the rest of her life with. She was more wildly attracted to him than ever before, and she knew she had to do something to control the impulses she felt. He clearly returned the feelings, and she was sure that their love would stem from a strong, mutual bond of irresistible adoration and friendship.

The rest of the evening passed in a happy haze of laughter, shared dreams, vows, and some of the most delicious food east of the great river. The future opened up to both of them as one enormous, spellbinding adventure that they would be taking together, as they embarked down a time-worn path that all lovers before them had taken through the ages. They both wished that the night would go on forever, and they knew that no matter what path loomed before them, no roadblock would ever separate them nor erase the cherished bliss of those unforgettable hours.

No sooner had they left and were outside in his car than they were again trailed by the same two men in a dark sedan. This time, the two young lovers noticed them during a series of turns when they were followed too closely in a way that could not have been explained as mere coincidences.

Allison asked, "Is there any reason you know of why you might be followed?"

"None," he said, observing the car in his rear view mirror.

She sighed and said, "I was afraid of that."

"Who do you think they are?"

"Have you ever heard of the Memphis Mafia?"

"Yeah. There've been rumors about some men who seem to be moving into the music business here."

"They may be following me."

He scrutinized them again in his rear view mirror. As they neared a freeway exit ramp, he said, "Watch this . . . ."

Without touching his brakes, he allowed gravity to slow his car's speed by about ten miles per hour, and then as he was about to pass the exit and the sedan was nearly on his bumper, he suddenly swung the steering wheel to the right and swerved off the freeway and down the ramp so abruptly that the sedan was unable to follow. The last they saw of the sedan was when the vehicle became ensnared in traffic that snaked far away from them into the distance.

Chapter Twenty-One

Sunday arrived like an unopened Christmas gift, a day that promised to be one of the most memorable in Allison's life. She spent hours being groomed for her appearance at the AIM Awards, including two hours at a hair salon to have her long red hair teased into luscious waves. All the while, she was more anxious about the *The Ed Sullivan Show* broadcast than her own moment in the spotlight.

Preparations for the live broadcast were in full swing early Sunday morning before dawn. Karen's photo mural had been set up in the WFBB-TV lobby, and the studio had been carefully staged so that the band would be juxtaposed against a background that depicted a long line of male guitar players shown only in dark silhouettes against a contrasting backdrop of blazing light. The stunning visual effect had been calculated to set the band's image as an iconic example of current Rock 'n' Roll singers that were sweeping radio airwaves. They knew they would have only three minutes to cement the image into the minds of all Americans, not to mention the annals of television history.

Although WFBB-TV had locked down their building to prevent outsiders from infiltrating the broadcast, Allison and Karen were allowed in due to their involvement with the band, but once they had offered their advice, they quietly hovered on the sidelines behind the cameras and let the professional technicians take over. Allison looked magnificent, even though she had not yet dressed in her new evening gown, which was hanging in one of the studio dressing rooms. She would change clothes there, right after the broadcast, and then dash to the Peabody Hotel in time to make her grand entrance.

The entire morning, the director rehearsed the cameramen and the band together in order to get their positions and movements timed with pinpoint accuracy. So much work for a mere fleeting moment of time on television! Since the broadcast would be live, every element had to be perfect. Four cameras with different lenses glided back and forth in front of and in the midst of the band, picking up their performance from a variety of angles that would give the broadcast a profound visual flair. They hoped people would talk about their achievement for years to come.

By mid-day, everyone took a well-deserved lunch break outside in the nippy air. A fenced patio behind the studio played host to a weenie roast of hotdogs with all the trimmings. There were even marshmallows to roast over the open fire pit. Everyone had hearty appetites, but what they really desired was to get back to work and make sure that they were doing their best for the one moment of time during which they would become the focal point of the entire industry.

After lunch, the band rehearsed their song several more times, and then the real fun began. As the clock inched toward evening, every member of the band except their lead singer submitted to all new haircuts. The studio's hairdresser carefully cut and combed their hair into a pompadour style that had just become all the rage with high school boys. She achieved the look by using generous amounts of pomade on their coifs to elevate their hair in front and give them a "duck's tail" in the back. They were all outfitted in new tight blue jeans with the cuffs rolled up on the outside of matching black patent leather motorcycle boots, and their outfits were topped by tight white t-shirts and black leather motorcycle jackets with chrome zippers that glistened under the glaring lights. Their look was planned to contrast with the lead singer, who was dressed in a shocking gold lamé suit that would reflect the glare of spotlights with his every movement.

Allison and Karen took positions in the director's booth, where he and a couple of other men sat hunched over an electronic board covered with dials and a bevy of monitors that showed every camera angle. They went over their cue sheets, repeatedly discussing each camera and when they would cut from one person to another. Allison and Karen could see the stage through the plate glass window separating them, and they could clearly see the band's image on each monitor.

By six thirty, everyone in the studio was on pins and needles and their heartbeats were all pounding in unison. The singer and the band took their positions on their marks on the stage beneath the hot lights. The director called for one more run-through as a dress rehearsal, and when they went through the song, every technical element clicked off with clock-like precision.

During a network station break, an announcer appeared on screen. "Ladies and gentlemen, an historic event will be taking place tonight. Coming to you live on *The Ed Sullivan Show* and broadcasting from Memphis, Tennessee . . . ."

No one in the studio actually heard him announce the name of the singer or the title of their hit record that was selling out in record stores each day as fast as new stock arrived, even though the announcer's words were piped in to every room in the building through the loudspeaker system. They had become too excited to soak in the announcement, having worked so hard all day to arrive at that one moment in time. They all became lost in the giddy moment. Even some of the men were misty-eyed, knowing that the public was being informed for the first time about the momentous event that would soon occur within the tiny studio that had become, for the hour, the heartbeat of Memphis.

The makeup lady had to rush onstage to mop the brows of the band, which were sweating beneath the heat of the floodlights, as the clock on the studio wall inched closer to the top of the hour.

The hairdresser also came out on stage and joined her to fuss with the lead singer's hair. "It's the light and the heat!" she complained. "It keeps making the front come loose and this one lock won't stay in place!"

"Jus' leave it, ma'm. Thanks for your concern, but it'll probably come down when I start moving around anyway," he said.

The director leaned into a microphone and said over the loudspeaker, "He's the boss. Leave the curl. The girls in Iowa will love it when their boyfriends imitate it tomorrow."

One technician on the telephone with the network shouted, "Ratings are going up! It's as if people all over the nation are turning their sets to the network in anticipation of their appearance!"

Every eye would soon see them. They were under the glare of national scrutiny! Outside, the first car with fans careened into a parking space. Out jumped a flock of teenagers, who ran to the studio entrance. Within another minute, several more cars arrived and more young people piled out. One girl ran to a telephone booth outside the studio, probably to call her friends, who would call their friends, who would then call their friends. The studio doors were opened to admit them all until the lobby filled up with fans.

By five minutes before seven, Allison could stand the tension no longer. Although she and Karen were off to one side of the control booth and not a part of the presentation, they were so in the thick of things that every movement of every person tugged at her nerves. They were mere minutes away from the moment when network editors would switch to the live feed from their studio.

A camera had been positioned on the far side of the lobby to pick up a few seconds of footage during the introduction. Nearly a hundred people, young and old, had suddenly converged and surrounded the camera that was pointed squarely on the cardboard cutout Karen had put together.

The director kept watching the clock in the control room. The hands seemed to have frozen at three minutes to seven and would not move, but then the big hand suddenly jumped to two minutes before seven.

"Two minutes . . . ." he announced in his microphone.

In the lobby, an assistant who was to hold up one of the band's 45 rpm singles close to the camera lens and then pull the record aside on cue took his position. He raised the record up to the lens. The cameraman focused.

Inside the control room, the image of the record appeared on one of the monitors, ready for the director to cut to the shot.

Allison took a deep breath and looked anxiously at Karen.

Karen nodded toward the studio floor and whispered, "See how calm he is?"

"I wish I was!" Allison whispered back fretfully.

She looked at him, standing there composed and unruffled, and then he looked up and saw her. He waved at her, and then loosed his hands from the guitar dangling on a strap around his neck and pointed to his ring finger and then back to her.

"My promise ring!" Allison whispered to Karen. "He wants to know if I've got it on!"

She raised her hand and pointed to the ring. He saw and smiled.

"Sixty seconds!" the director said.

One of the monitors on the control board showed what was airing on the network. The opening credits for *The Ed Sullivan Show* came on along with the theme music. After twenty seconds, the shot dissolved to the New York Theater where the famous host appeared on stage in front of huge curtains. "Thank you, ladies and gentlemen," he began. "Welcome to our show. We have a really big show for you tonight, beginning with our introduction of The King of Rock 'n' Roll, the singer who has made blue suede shoes one of the most popular icons of the new music scene . . . ."

Inside the Memphis control booth, the director said into his microphone "Five seconds!"

Outside the studio in the lobby, the crowd began to cheer wildly. No one heard the rest of Sullivan's announcement, but an assistant cued the cameraman, who kept the 45 rpm record sharply in focus for a few seconds before panning up to the uproarious crowd gathered in front of the photo cutout of the band. Everyone heard the band strike the opening notes of their song and a crescendo of hoots and hollers overfilled the lobby.

"Cut to camera one," the director said.

Allison and Karen watched the network monitor, as a full shot suddenly appeared on the screen showing the entire band. The director then cut to a succession of long shots that showed the entire band as they sang in front of a striking backdrop of silhouetted guitar-playing men, followed by medium shots that honed-in on various band members, close-ups of the lead singer with one curl hanging over his sweating brow, moving camera shots, and even an extreme close-up of the frets on the lead guitar.

Allison wept. She could not take her eyes off the network monitor, where the details taking place unknown to the rest of the world yet all around her were blended into a technically perfect presentation the way people at home in their living rooms were seeing the broadcast at that exact same moment.

The entire three minutes passed too quickly. *It's over?* she thought, when she saw the band taking a bow. *Twenty hours of work by seventy-two people just passed like it was only a few seconds?*

"You were great!" she heard the director shout through his microphone.

Allison knew that what she had just witnessed had made a colossal impact. There were some Norwegian jugglers on *The Ed Sullivan Show* now, but she could hear pandemonium erupting in the lobby just on the other side of the wall behind where she and Karen were standing. The band had not only done good, they had broken through an unseen barrier between young and old, launched a trend that might not change for decades, and set in place an image for themselves that could forever imprint their look and sound on the minds of millions. She and Karen were so overjoyed and relieved that they hugged each other.

"I've got to congratulate him!" Allison nearly screamed to Karen.

"And then go change clothes," Karen said. "People are already gathering at the Peabody Hotel for the AIM Awards. You both have to make your grand entrance!"

Chapter Twenty-Two

The AIM Awards was the big event of the year, and Allison was his girl. She had to look better than a movie star for him, for her father, for Karen, for herself, and for all that she had promised to herself during those long years in college when she labored alone late at night studying for exams, dreaming of the future, and praying that her ambitions were not in vain. She'd always hoped that one day she might win a major award for an important achievement that would prove to everyone she was more than a hairbrush in a cast of thousands, that she was an outstanding contributor to the advertising industry. She was also determined to look better than Sharon Eaton.

We should be the most striking couple on the red carpet, she thought, *even though Sharon vowed that she'd grab the spotlight from everyone and show up wearing a diamond-studded Coco Chanel gown.* Allison emerged wearing a ravishing red satin damask formal that featured a strapless sweetheart neckline on a fitted bodice that glittered with diamond-looking stones. The tightly-fitted waist and horizontal pleats accented her perfect figure. The final touch was her choice of long white over-the-elbow gloves that would have given Rita Hayworth a run for her money. The overall effect along with her red hair pulled to the right and gently cascading over one bare shoulder wowed the crew. Several of them stung the air with a rowdy chorus of complimentary whistles when she passed, but no one was more charmed than the man whose promise ring she proudly wore.

He met her wearing a smart dark blue suit and matching fedora, a sharp contrast to his glitzy stage attire. They paused inside the door that opened to the overcrowded lobby.

"Thank you for being with me during the show," he said. "Did you approve of everything?"

"Approve? You were so wonderful I cried so hard my makeup ran down my face!"

He kissed her, softly at first, and then passionately. His hands were tightly holding her waist, and he held his lips to hers as if he wanted them to merge into one. No one saw the two of them, although a noisy throng waited just on the other side of the door. He had endured the microscopic scrutiny of penetrating cameras, and soon, she would undergo intense analysis by the curious and perhaps envious, but for those precious seconds, they were alone in the world and free to give themselves over to the deep passions surging through their blood. Allison easily imagined that Heaven had opened up and angels were tickling her with their wings.

"I love you, Allison," she heard him say.

"I love you, too," she replied in a throaty whisper.

They kissed again, but this time he was not satisfied with merely kissing her lips. He kissed the soft, sensitive side of her neck and the tender folds of her ear, while she gave in to the temptation to kiss his chin and cheeks.

Finally he murmured, "Maybe we should go?"

Allison caught her breath and gazed searchingly into the deep pools of his languid eyes. "First, I have to tell you something . . . ."

"Yes?"

"You have cherry red lipstick all over your face."

He quickly withdrew a handkerchief and dabbed at his cheeks.

On the other side of the door, rowdy admirers had gotten wind of the fact that he was soon to emerge among them, and they began chanting for him to come out. To everyone's intense delight, the door swung open and they responded with a raucous chorus of cheers. Allison emerged alone, but she teased them by extending one white-gloved arm behind her holding onto an unseen man's hand. Then, after a moment of sublime suspense, he stepped out, kissed her again, and they faced an ovation of flashing light bulbs, catcalls, whistles, and applause. They were instantly besieged and barely able to navigate through the crowd to the exit. Outside, studio personnel had thoughtfully drawn up her car, which sat idling with both doors open. They took her Chevy convertible because the car was new, but he drove. They made their exit feeling like newlyweds embarking on a honeymoon.

Phillip Samuels had grown bored standing around the huge Peabody Hotel indoor pool, where Sharon Eaton was holding court with all the pomp of a Queen awaiting her coronation. True to her vow, she had arrived draped in a stunning black strapless floor-length evening dress of lace over silk with a ruffle bottom that fit tight around her lower legs and swished when she moved. She stood planted in a strategic position at the center of the atrium right beside the pool, which had been decorated with six huge bouquets of red roses nestled in greenery that cuddled flickering candles and floated languorously across the glass-like water. Fichus trees had been placed every few feet around the edge of the pool, and they were decorated with hidden lights. No less than a small crowd of people sipping from long-stemmed wine glasses surrounded Sharon, while she chattered self-consciously about herself, her nomination for Rookie of the Year, her ascension to Vice Presidency of Star Records, her merger with B&B Marketing, her former successes in Nashville, and her current ambitions in Memphis.

Phillip turned to Wiley Pearson, one of his associates, and said, "Thank God this room has fifteen-foot ceilings. At least I can breathe in here. Otherwise, the atmosphere would be suffocating! There's too much *hot air!*" he said sarcastically, nodding toward Sharon.

"I take it you don't have a high opinion of the First Lady of Marketing?"

Phillip had rejected the prissy wine in long-stemmed glasses and instead clutched a highball glass. He took a big swig of his gin and tonic and bitterly replied, "If she's the First Lady, then I'm Vice President Richard Nixon!"

"She's getting all the attention tonight," Wiley said. "I overheard her say that her dress was embedded with real diamonds in the front and back."

"Really? I might dance with her later then. I'll see if I can't pluck a few of them off. She owes me more than that after practically seizing control of my company. See that goofball standing right next to her?"

"The tall Italian-looking guy with the dark hair and sideburns?"

"That's Guido Rizzo. Doing business with his family is like bartering with the Devil. They don't give in to anything! They forced me to give up controlling interest!"

"Why did you?"

"I didn't have a choice. They made me an offer I couldn't refuse, if you know what I mean."

"Oh. That sounds ominous. And speaking of menacing, who are those guys loitering around the back area over there? Security?"

Phillip glanced where Wiley was looking and muttered, "I don't know. I wouldn't be surprised if they're FBI."

"Surely not. Why would they be here?"

"Why not? They're everywhere. Maybe they're guarding the gold-plated awards. Who cares?"

Indeed, beside the lectern the awards committee had outlaid a table draped with a white cloth that was adorned with the six annual awards the committee intended to give out that night, but the intimidating-looking huddle of dark-suited men were nowhere near the display. Would-be winners meandered by the ostentatious outlay and ogled the prized statuettes, but no guards stood over them.

Another small cluster of men loitered not far from them, press photographers and journalists, who had been waiting entirely too long for their restless energies. They had already snapped photos of everyone arriving at the party, and nothing remained for them to do but wait for the actual awards so they could grab their last pictures and leave.

A pianist had quietly taken his place at a grand piano on the far side of the pool, but just before he began to softly play, Elizabeth Worthington, a heavy-set arts patron with Rex, her dour husband and benefactor, entered the party room in a rush, excitedly making a beeline to Phillip. She grabbed Phillip's arm and excitedly chattered, "You'll never guess who just drove up outside at the valet stand! It's none other than Allison Webster, one of the two nominated for Best Print Ad Campaign. She looks like a princess in a stunning crimson gown! And guess who's with her—none other than that dear boy everyone's talking about who created such a sensation on *The Ed Sullivan Show* tonight, the record singer making all the waves! Allison got him that booking, you know! I understand that the two of them are an item!"

Wiley nodded in agreement. "Everyone in the lobby's talking about him."

"She's with him! He's divine, and I've just got to get his autograph! He's on your label, Phillip. You should have told me he was coming here tonight!"

Elizabeth was not the only person buzzing about the "dear boy" everyone was talking about. Once they had driven up under the porte cochere, news of the singing sensation's arrival in their midst quickly spread from the doorman to the valet to the bellmen and to the front desk clerks. Even the housekeepers, kitchen help, and banquet servers were immediately informed, as gossip of his unexpected appearance spread like a wildfire throughout the hotel.

Tittle-tattle voices such as Elizabeth's had also carried the extraordinarily exciting report through chit chat whispered breathlessly from ear to ear among everyone attending the poolside party, easily sweeping away all conversations about Sharon Eaton, talk that had already grown stale. Without a single effort on Allison's part, her mere presence in the hotel at that moment with the Man of the Hour caused such a stir that news of their impending entrance quickly reached Sharon and Guido.

Guido frowned and said to Sharon in an undertone, "This won't do at all!"

Sharon cupped her hand over his ear and replied so quietly that no one else could hear, "Do something to distract the photographers. This night isn't about *her*. It's about *me*!"

A young, white-gloved and tuxedoed server standing near the group had already overheard that her idol had arrived, and she was breathlessly awaiting his appearance in the flesh. She took her eyes off the guests and stared in anticipation at the double doors. When the doors finally opened and she saw a flash of movement, she forgot herself, nearly dropped her silver tray on which several long-stemmed wine glasses were precariously balanced, and screamed, "It's *him*!"

Chapter Twenty-Three

The bored photographers jumped as if someone had just yelled "Fire!" They rushed to surround the red carpet and bombard the arriving couple with one flash bulb burst after another as they jockeyed each other to shoot as many photographs as possible. The photographer for the *Memphis Daily Appeal* was in such a rush to replace the spent bulb in his camera that he dropped an entire box of spare bulbs. The bulbs popped like gun shots, and in the excitement, no one noticed one of the dark-suited men in the back of the room react like a knee jerk and reach inside his coat as if to withdraw a weapon. The excitement over the arriving couple obliterated all thoughts of anything else.

As if on cue, the piano player began playing the opening bars of the hit song that had just caused such a stir on *The Ed Sullivan Show*.

Elizabeth Worthington beamed and cooed to Phillip Samuels, "Darling, did you put him up to accompanying Allison Webster here tonight? You're so clever! Not that she needs anything to attract attention to herself, mind you, but what a coup for you!"

"He's definitely one of our rising stars," Phillip replied proudly.

"And hasn't she done a sensational job getting him on national television? I can tell she'll be a force to reckon with in the coming year!"

Everyone who had been surrounding Sharon was so entranced by the arriving couple that they inadvertently drifted away from her to ogle, a detail she thought equal to the historic explosion of the Hindenburg blimp. In one fell swoop, she suddenly became stepsister Drizella to Allison's Cinderella, and even tall handsome Guido Rizzo, her date for the evening, was no match for Allison's Prince Charming.

Since Sharon and Guido suddenly had been abandoned and no one stood beside them other than two of their cronies, she seethed. Through gritted teeth, she asked Guido, "How much cash do you have on you?"

"A few hundred. Why?"

"When no one's looking, pay off the *Memphis Daily Appeal's* photographer to stop taking pictures of her for the rest of the evening! I won't have it!"

Allison was not normally one to make a late entrance to an invitation only event, but because of the unusual circumstances of the day, she could not help arriving later than others. At that, they had entered the party well ahead of the actual start of the awards portion of the program.

Once the hubbub somewhat subsided, Guido quietly drew the *Daily News'* photographer aside and discretely tended to Sharon's demand.

The photographer took the cash wad that Guido surreptitiously slipped him, but he said, "Look, buddy, I'll take a few more pictures of Sharon Eaton, but it's about nine o'clock now, and we've got a ten o'clock deadline for the morning paper. They're not going to hold the presses for me. I'm leaving at nine thirty or as soon as we get pictures of the winners, whichever comes first!"

Guido patted him on the back. "Just keep the cameras aimed on Sharon as much as you can. Besides, I think they're about to hand out the awards."

Allison did not have to meander around the room to mingle with others. For once, they sidled up to her because they were only too eager to rub elbows with the genuine star accompanying her. For his part, he gallantly deflected attention away from himself. Every time someone began plying him with questions, he turned the conversation back to Allison and her work as one of the community's most outstanding advertising and marketing executives. When he noticed Phillip Samuels, he asked, "Would you excuse me for just a minute? I'd like to speak to him."

"Of course!" she said.

Marshall Wells came up to her accompanying a charming blonde she had never met. "Allison, I'd like you to meet Meredith Adams. Meredith, this is Allison Webster. She's nominated for Best Print Ad Campaign."

"Pleased to meet you," Allison said. "It looks like the party's off to a great start!"

Marshall smiled brightly and agreed. "I think so, too, now that you're here. Frankly, we were all getting a little sick of watching everyone buzzing around Sharon Eaton like flies. She's made sure that everyone including the reporters knows that her black ruffle bottom dress was designed by Coco Channel. Frankly, I think it makes her look like Morticia Addams in those *New Yorker* cartoons."

"Oh Marshall!" Meredith laughed.

"Now that everyone has been welcomed, I can relax and spend some time with the people I'd like to be with most. You look more beautiful than I've ever seen you, Allison!"

"Your gown *is* exquisite, Allison," Meredith said.

"Thank you, and so is yours."

They were suddenly interrupted by the sound of a wine glass being tapped next to the microphone in front of the lectern. They looked up to see Alan Brooks, comptroller for B&B Marketing and AIM Awards Committee Chairperson, at the lectern. "Ladies and Gentlemen," he spoke into the microphone, "Welcome to the 10th Annual AIM Awards."

Allison felt a strong warm hand gently take hold of her elbow. She was sensed the faint yet delightfully familiar aroma of Lentheric Musketeer Shave Lotion Cologne, and she heard the smooth sexy male voice that only two hours earlier had sung through millions of television sets whisper, "Your moment is now." He kissed her softly on her neck once again, so deftly that the fleeting second passed unnoticed by others, yet so sincerely that she could not help but swoon. She was in ecstasy just being near him again, and her body heat rose several degrees, as always happened when he was so close to her that he left her bedazzled.

All eyes turned toward Alan Brooks, but Allison wanted only to let her eyes linger on the face of the man who thrilled her more than anyone or anything else in the world. Suddenly, winning an award seemed meaningless. She did not care if she went home empty handed. All that mattered was that the two of them were together.

Alan continued his introduction. "Why is this year's award presentation held in the Peabody Hotel's pool atrium, some of you have asked? I can assure you that it's not because we intend to play water polo afterward. Our theme is 'The Sky's The Limit,' thus the glass-roof atrium locale. The pool water signifies the world and the public at large, and if you'll notice, we've floated six red rose bouquets in the water. Those bouquets represent our six winners. The color red symbolizes your passion for your work, and the flame denotes your fire for excellence. We'll now begin the presentation of those six awards . . . ."

Allison had to pay attention to the speaker. Doting lovingly on the face that was only inches from hers, gazing with longing into his misty eyes that would not stop adoring her, savoring the endearing crinkle that turned up one side of his mouth, and delighting in seeing the return of that little loose curl that always seemed to reappear like an old friend on his forehead would have to wait for another hour. She forced herself to look away from him and at the speaker, but her attention accidentally snagged momentarily on Sharon, who she saw take a deep breath and unconsciously lick her lips as if she was starving to finally be satiated by whatever was about to happen. When Sharon turned to fully face the speaker, Allison noticed that she had a little bit of trouble maneuvering the heavy folds of her ruffle bottom dress. Guido had to catch her at her elbow and steady her from actually tripping on the frivolous fabric.

"Our first award is for Outstanding Achievement in Television Commercials," Alan said. He opened a sealed envelope and then read, "Nominees are Pauline Bush and Norma Lawrence. And the winner is Pauline Bush for her dazzling series created for Memphis Ford!"

While generous applause accompanied Pauline as she approached the lectern, an obscure rear door quietly opened and FBI agents Wilkins and Walker unobtrusively slipped in and blended into the crowd. Pauline was handed a long-stem red rose and her award, and as all eyes were on her, she wiped away a tear and graciously bowed.

"Our second award is for Most Creative Radio Commercials." Alan opened an envelope and read, "Nominees are Xavier Bayne and George Larkin . . . and the winner is George Larkin for his unforgettable Memphis Philharmonic campaign."

Bighearted cheers and clapping escorted George as he maneuvered through the crowd to accept his golden statuette. Alan pinned a red rose onto his lapel, and the throng was so enamored of George that all eyes were on him as he waved thankfully to them and photographers captured the moment on film. No one got so much as a glimpse through the shuttered sun windows in the back of flashing red lights on several police cars that had just pulled up.

"Our next award is for Best Billboards," Alan said. He opened an envelope and read, "Nominees are Helene Hawkins and Genevive Costello. The winner is Helene Hawkins for the Duck and Cover public service announcement billboards everyone's seen all over Memphis!"

An outpouring of appreciation buoyed Helene as she hugged her husband and then sailed through her friends to the lectern. She nearly knocked Alan over when she hugged him, and then when he handed her the award, she hugged the statuette as if the award was a jewel straight out of Tutankhamen's treasures. When Alan handed her a long-stem red rose, she comically held it in her mouth while posing for her portrait. Everyone was so amused by her euphoric antics that they were completely unaware of Walker and Wilkins giving brief but firm orders to their counterparts, the bevy of dark-suited unknown men that had shadowed the entire proceedings.

"Our fourth award is the coveted Preeminent Point of Purchase Posters," Alan remarked. He opened another envelope and smiled broadly. "Nominees are David Darrington and Paul Kelly. The award goes to B&B advertising's own Paul Kelly for the Del Valle artwork! Congratulations, Paul!"

Kindly kudos and catcalls erupted when Paul fairly leapt from the midst of a cadre of his pals to the lectern. Alan pinned a red rose on his lapel, proudly bestowed his award upon him, and profusely patted him on the back. They posed shaking hands for the photographers, and while their flash bulbs were going off, a grim-faced Walker and stern-jawed Wilkins maneuvered slowly through the throng with their eyes steeled on one knot of party goers.

"And our next to last award celebrates the Best Print Ad Campaign of the Year," Alan stated. "Nominees are Allison Webster and Mel Weinberg!"

Two of the dark-suited men took positions in front of the atrium's double doors. Two others blocked the side entrance, and the last two silently obstructed the server's entrance, while agents Wilkins and Walker covertly withdrew a pair of handcuffs from their pockets.

Allison felt the strong hand clutching hers raise her hand to his lips. He did not care if anyone was watching him, as he quietly kissed her hand. "You're going to win!" he said in a voice soft and low.

Alan tore open an envelope and said, "I know that many of you have especially been waiting to hear who the winner is for this award. Our esteemed nominees this year represent the best that our industry offers. I congratulate both of you, but the winner is . . . ."

Chapter Twenty-Four

"... Allison Webster!"

A happy roar of voices erupted, and their thundering applause nearly deafened Allison. She heard shouts of best wishes from everyone surrounding her and instantly became engulfed by her overjoyed friends and associates.

Agent Wilkins reached for Agent Walker's arm and stopped him from moving further forward. The ovation kept anyone from hearing him whisper "Let her have her moment of glory. It's the last she'll have for a long time to come."

Allison could not hold back tears from filling her eyes, but she glided through the wall of bodies and reached Alan with a smile on her face. He handed her a long-stem red rose and gave her the statuette that symbolized her well-deserved achievement.

Alan waited for the happy hollering to die down, but the clamor continued unabated. Allison had to dab at her eyes with one of her white-gloved fingers, and the photographers captured that heart-felt moment in a volley of flash bulbs.

Finally, Alan had to continue on despite the spirited shouting and applause. Allison knew that she had her moment of glory, and she was considerate enough of the proceedings to selflessly step away so that the awards presentation could continue.

Wilkins nudged Walker and said, "Now."

"Our last award," Alan announced, "is for Rookie of the Year. Nominees are Janice Jennings and Sharon Eaton."

Sharon took a deep breath. Seeing that her path to the lectern was blocked by a horde of people she did not know, she began taking a step forward as Alan opened the final envelope.

"And the winner is Janice Jennings . . . ."

Janice screamed in excited animation.

". . . for her Ace Department Store campaign!"

Sharon thought she had not heard right and shot a stung glare at Alan that would have bested Julius Caesar upon seeing Brutus lunge at him with his knife. Suddenly, Wilkins reached through the crowd and grabbed her arm. Sharon swung around doubly shocked as her heel caught again in her ruffle bottom dress. She screamed, lost her footing, began to topple backward and grabbed at one of the fichus trees, but the potted plant instantly snapped in half. She plunged over the edge of the pool and hit the water with an enormous splash that splattered a wave six feet into the air and doused nearly everyone nearby.

As she sank beneath the water, photographers swung around and scrambled poolside to snap pictures of her. She momentarily resurfaced from directly under one of the floral bouquets, but unfortunately, the roses were on top of her head and the drenched greenery draped over each side of her face like hound dog ears. She spewed a stream of water from her mouth just as the humiliating moment was instantly recorded by all seven cameramen.

"Don't just stand there!" Sharon bellowed at Guido before sinking again. They saw nothing on the surface of the water but bubbles, but then she broke through for another second, screaming and gurgling "Help me!" before submerging again.

Agent Wilkins glared at Guido and demanded, "Get her out of there!"

"*I'm* not going in there!" Guido retorted. "This is a Christian Dior suit I'm wearing! The water's only four and a half feet deep. She can stand if she'll just get a hold of herself!"

One of the other FBI officers shoved through the crowd carrying a pool net on a fifteen-foot stick. He lowered the net into the water and extended the stick out as far as the pole could reach. Sharon clutched at the net and he reeled her in like an ocean tuna fish. Three men had to pluck her gagging from the water.

She had lost both her shoes and stood dripping in a puddle. Her once bouffant ruffle bottom was now flattened sopping wet and resembled mermaid fins. Agent Wilkins slapped handcuffs on her. "You're under arrest."

Sharon stood there stunned, soaked, shivering, humiliated, enraged over the galling loss of her award, and livid at Guido for refusing to come to her aid. Disgusted, she shrieked at Wilkins, "What is this?"

Wilkins replied, "You're under arrest for racketeering charges, including conspiracy to commit extortion and bribery."

Walker deftly snapped handcuffs on Guido's wrists, adding, "You're also under arrest for racketeering charges including conspiracy to commit extortion, bribery, threat involving murder, kidnapping, gambling, arson, robbery, money laundering, and loan sharking."

As shocked partygoers began to gasp and back away from the stunning scene unfolding right before their eyes, the opportunistic newspaper reporters and photographers scrambled to surround the action like bloodhounds cornering a fox. They scrawled down on their notepads the charges the FBI men had just read, and added to their shots of Sharon floundering in the water like a drowning rat some new pictures of her and Guido captured, shackled in handcuffs, and surrounded by FBI men.

Although Allison and others were discrete in hiding their amusement over Sharon's unceremonious fall from grace, Marshall Wells, who had always thought of her the way he thought of sitting on a porcupine, could not contain his laughter. Sharon was within earshot, so he snorted, "Well, Sharon . . . I knew you wanted to make a big splash in Memphis, but isn't this overdoing things, even for you?"

The *Memphis Daily Appeal's* photographer nudged through the men surrounding Guido and stuffed the $100 bribe back into his coat pocket. "Keep your cash, bud," he said. "These pictures I've got of you and her will be worth a hundred times that once they get picked up by API! Tomorrow morning, the whole country will know about this!"

Sharon saw Allison grinning at what Marshall and the photographer had said, but in her terror and confusion, she assumed that she was gloating and snickering at her, so she screeched, "I hate you Allison Webster! You plotted this! It's all your fault! I'll get even with you!"

Allison could only smile and shake her head with pity. "I only wish I could have, Sharon, but you once told me that you were going to be 'part of the picture, here, now, and forever after,' and I guess these newspaper photographers have helped you achieve what you wanted. I expect those pictures *will* be in the papers, here, now, and forever after!"

The site of Sharon and Guido being led out in handcuffs certainly gave the AIM Awards a memorable high point that everyone talked about the rest of the evening until the affair officially ended.

The hood of Allison's new convertible reflected the bright Memphis moon, as they drove away that night. She snuggled her head on the shoulder of the one man she hoped to know and love for the rest of her life, while her AIM award nestled in her lap like a sleepy child. The entire day and night had been one for their memory books. Just before they heard his hit song on the radio, a disc jockey announced that the overnight Nielsen ratings for *The Ed Sullivan Show* had skyrocketed to more than 80% of the television viewing audience, an unheard-of record. His career had launched to a new level, and neither of them yet had any way of knowing where that success would take him . . . or her.

He was humming along with his own voice on the airwaves, but then he said, "Isn't it funny how we . . . ." He stopped, as if he was lost in thought.

". . . can't help falling in love?"

"You read my mind. I love you, Allison. I want you to be with me from now on. Do you think you could love me forever?"

Allison felt a rush of feeling well up inside her. "I feel like I've known you forever. It seems like forever that I've been aching inside because I couldn't believe I could be yours or that you could really be mine. I guess some things are meant to be."

He put his fingers to her lips. "Don't say anything more."

He pulled the car over to the side of the road and stopped. They were alone on the lonely stretch of highway and nothing but the moon accompanied them, seeming to smile down at the two of them like an approving old acquaintance. He turned the volume down on the radio and said, "I don't want to compete with him." He put his arms around Allison and drew her so close they could feel each other's heart beat. His embrace felt warm and strong.

She looked up into his eyes and they kissed. His lips were tender and searching, and she responded to him in a way that took on a thrilling, new meaning. She secretly thought, *I feel like we've both climbed to a mountain top tonight. Where on earth can we go from here?*

As if he read her mind, he said, "We're taking the band to a bunch of other cities for the next few weeks, including a few gigs on the west coast so we can grab some more TV work. Wouldn't it be great if you could come with me?"

Allison thought for only a second. "I'm overdue for a vacation."

He grinned broadly as he shifted the gears. "I was hoping you'd say something like that. I think you look more beautiful than a movie star tonight. I can only imagine how great you'll look when we get to Hollywood and spend some time under the palm trees at the beach."

He carefully glided the car back onto the road. As they listened to the rest of his hit song on the radio and the wind tickled that stubborn little loose curl that seemed to permanently reside on his forehead, Allison hugged him affectionately and thought, *What could be more wonderful than being under palm trees and sunshine with the man I love? We've got a future together and a whole lifetime to explore all the possibilities that love has to offer!*

The End

About Carol Dunitz

Carol Dunitz is a writer, composer, actor, and producer with a distinguished career in marketing, writing, and performance. Carol ran a marketing agency, The Last Word LLC, for many years during which time she produced numerous advertising and PR campaigns, wrote speeches for high level executives, and spoke professionally around the country. She is the author of numerous books including *Already Spoken For, One Hungry Child,* and *Louder Than Thunder*, which received over two dozen positive reviews in national and regional media. Carol is currently touring in *Bernhardt on Broadway*, a one-woman musical about Sarah Bernhardt for which she wrote the music, script and lyrics. Carol is also working on a new musical about Mary Todd Lincoln. She has a Doctorate in Speech Communication and Theatre. Carol lives in Ann Arbor, MI, USA.

About David W. Menefee

Pulitzer-nominated author David W. Menefee began his writing career with the *Dallas Times Herald* and the *Dallas Morning News* before striking out on his own as a freelance writer and film historian. His *Richard Barthelmess: A Life in Pictures* was named one of the Top 10 Books of the Year by Thomas Gladysz in the *San Francisco Examiner*. In 2010, *George O'Brien: A Man's Man in Hollywood* and *"Otay!" The Billy "Buckwheat" Thomas Story* were popular hits. In 2011, his *Wally: The True Wallace Reid Story* was nominated for a Pulitzer and named one of the Best Silent Film Books of the Year along with his *The Rise and Fall of Lou-Tellegen*. His Margot Cranston detective series continues to please an ever-growing worldwide audience. David lives in Dallas, Texas, USA.

Bernhardt on Broadway
The New Musical

"Bernhardt on Broadway by Carol Dunitz captures the character of Sarah Bernhardt and serves up her divine spirit on a plate decorated with toe-tapping tunes." –David W. Menefee.

"The script brought Bernhardt to life. Catchy music. Many went out of their way to let me know how much they enjoyed the show . . . even young people in their teens and twenties." -Kristine Swisher, Artistic Director Holland Theatre, Bellfontaine, Ohio.

"I was floored by the intimacy of the script. I felt like Madame Sarah was a close personal friend who was revealing secrets to me that she could not possibly share with anyone else. The music is divine." -Allen Nichols, Manager Maxims: The Nancy Goldberg Int'l Center, Chicago, Illinois.

"I was impressed by the amount of research for this show. Although I am French, I learned a lot about Sarah Bernhardt. I enjoyed the songs. Great voice!" -Monique Tranchevent, Paris/Chicago Sisters Cities Committee.

**For more information or to book the show:
Carol Dunitz 312.523.4774
CDunitz@BernhardtOnBroadway.com
www.BernharadtOnBroadway.com**

Louder Than Thunder

Written for ages 5 - 105, *Louder Than Thunder* is a beautifully illustrated parable about a CEO who calls in her three vice presidents to tell them she is about to step down and that one of them will succeed her. She has a riddle for them and whoever comes back with the best answer will be the next CEO. The riddle is: What is louder than thunder, as highly charged as lightning, and more powerful than the fierce North Wind?

Louder Than Thunder shares invaluable lessons on interpersonal communication through a series of vignettes. The reader is taken on a journey with the book's protagonist as she learns to deal with the world around her by carefully listening and observing. In the process, the reader comes to understand how to communicate more effectively in everyday interactions.

Book, Learning Guide, and CD available online at:
http://www.louderthanthunder.com/Products.html

Sweet Memories

Sweet Memories fades in on Mary Pickford, Owen Moore, and a dazzling all-star cast of celebrities in the enduring story of an indomitable girl's vision of victory and her mother's untiring endeavors to achieve those dreams no matter what the cost. After ten years of touring the back roads of Broadway, sixteen-year-old Mary, lovely as a spring rose, faces the greatest challenge of her life. Caught on a merry-go-round making movies, worldwide adulation elevates her onto an unsteady pedestal as The Biograph Girl, where labor and love mix like oil and water. Only Charlotte, her mother, stands by her side during the tempest of adoration, and only Owen abides in her heart. Together, they join a rowdy band of independent filmmakers in Cuba, but none of them suspect that they have unwittingly set sail on an explosive adventure that will take a lifetime to forget.

**Available in print and Kindle book editions.
Visit your favorite online bookseller,
or order from any book store.**

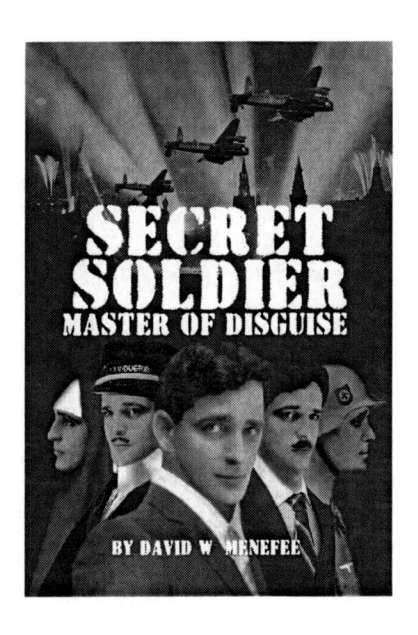

Secret Soldier, Master of Disguise

In David W. Menefee's brilliant new love story, a secret soldier lives up to the title "Master of Disguise," when terror strikes suddenly and Hitler's SS troops arrest his fiancé on the day they plan to furtively escape Nazi occupied Berlin. He believes that love, determination, and ingenuity can overcome all obstacles, and he lights the fuse for an epic, countdown battle of good against evil. Alone and stoic in the face of utter malevolence, he launches a bold, daring, and desperate plan to liberate her from the clutches of doom. Can his one-man army triumph against all odds and win in a war-torn world gone mad?

**Available in print and Kindle book editions.
Visit your favorite online bookseller,
or order from any book store.**

MARGOT CRANSTON
The Quest for the Jade Dragons

A wonderful wedding and honeymoon at Niagara Falls should bring a night of delight to remember forever, but when famous detective Margot Cranston attends, a party in paradise becomes a festivity with fear. Two priceless jade dragons promise power and riches for whoever possesses the famous twin figurines. The bride plans for them to bring joy to the world, but her enemy plots to gain power from the gems. Join Margot, her niece Amy, and her nephew Andy, for the reception near the rapids and famed waterfall, but prepare to be drawn into a whirlpool of intrigue on their death-defying quest for the jade dragons.

**Available in print and Kindle book editions.
Visit your favorite online bookseller,
or order from any book store.**

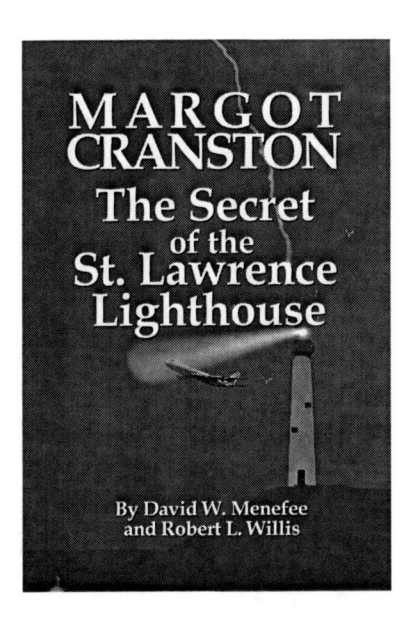

MARGOT CRANSTON
The Secret of the St. Lawrence Lighthouse

When detective Margot Cranston vacations in Montreal, a cruise ship sails into a crime-riddled nightmare. A ghastly ghost haunting an ancient lighthouse stirs trouble in the waters of the St. Lawrence River. Margot, her niece Amy, and her nephew Andy are ensnared in a weekend of trickery and intrigue that only an encounter with the phantom can resolve. Margot risks danger, deception, and her own death to unravel the secret of the St. Lawrence lighthouse.

**Available in print and Kindle book editions.
Visit your favorite online bookseller,
or order from any book store.**

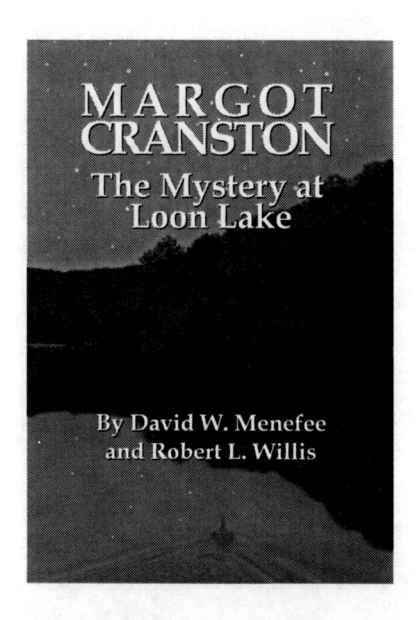

MARGOT CRANSTON
The Mystery at Loon Lake

Reuniting with old acquaintances should be great fun, but when famous detective Margot Cranston attends, a bash with friends becomes a crash with enemies. No one suspects evil to be lurking in the dark when a flash of lightning kills power at the party, but Margot lights a candle that ignites the fuse for one of the strangest cases in her mystery-solving career. Her investigation of a severed wire leads through dangerous warehouses and long-hidden rooms, as she unearths startling proof of a criminal ring. With help from her niece Amy and nephew Andy, Margot soon realizes that the Loon Lake shores harbor more than love and romantic hideaways. Join Margot on a weekend rendezvous with revenge, when a trail of clues throws her into troubled waters, as she unravels the shocking mystery at Loon Lake.

**Available in print and Kindle book editions.
Visit your favorite online bookseller,
or order through any bookstore.**

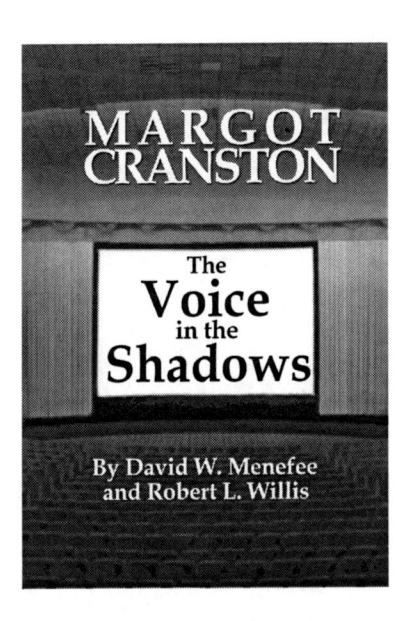

MARGOT CRANSTON
The Voice in the Shadows

Tinsletown becomes Terrorville when Margot visits friends in Hollywood. When she, her niece Amy, and her nephew Andy are stunned by the death of a silver screen legend, a spotlight falls on a lost will, a cryptic riddle, and a roster of villains that would make a casting director envious. Margot rolls out a red carpet of ruses to unearth a secret long buried in the dark Hollywood hills, and no one suspects that only a voice in the shadows knows the unscripted truth.

**Available exclusively in a Kindle book edition.
Visit your favorite online bookseller.**